The
TREASURE
With a
FACE

ISBN 978-1-7356643-8-5
September 2021

www.perpetuallightpublishing.com

The TREASURE With a FACE

JANEEN ZAIO

CONTENTS

Discussion Questions begin on page 241, and the glossary begins on page 261. Vocabulary words and their definitions can be found on JaneenZaio.com.

CHAPTER 1

TREASURE STORY OR MYTH?

The treasure is still out there. He left it for you. I could tell you where to find it right now, but it's better if you discover it yourself. My name is Eli, and I'd like to help you the way John helped me—both before and after he was put in a vat of boiling oil. Don't worry, surely that won't happen to you. And I'll spare you the experience of digging through maggot-filled garbage or crawling in glowing caves.

While some treasure hunters live within one day's walk of treasure, it remains undiscovered because they don't know what to look for. We won't let that happen. You may wonder how a treasure hunter born

3

in Galilee during the time of Jesus could possibly know that the treasure is located near your house. Let's just say that from my vantage point, I can see forever.

I always loved treasures but didn't officially become a treasure hunter until I was twelve years old. I remember the exact day because it was the second worst day of my life. At least up until that point.

It all started one morning as I stood in the forest watching boys chop firewood. I had gone out in search of wood to make a chest but stopped to watch them throwing an ax at a stump. It certainly wasn't the most efficient way to chop firewood, but perhaps they didn't live with an efficiency expert like I did.

They agreed to let me throw the ax when suddenly, I saw a traveler approaching. Many travelers used this road because it went from the Great Sea to the Sea of Galilee. Perhaps he'd bring me news of treasure—treasure of any variety—buried, sunken, plundered, paraded, or entombed.

As he got closer, I could see this was no ordinary traveler. He wore a turban on his head, and his white horse had a horn on its forehead. Those were telltale signs that the traveler was a Persian. I waved my arms to get his attention. Actually, first I dropped the ax near my feet, then I waved my arms.

The traveler kept going, so I chased after him. When he veered toward our Galilean village, I took a shortcut through a creek. I had only met a Persian once before, and he was a great storyteller, although I wasn't sure he always told the truth.

When I arrived at my village, I looked down the street to see if the traveler stopped at the market that stretched through the center of town. A horrible odor entered my nostrils. The stench was coming from across the street where a woman was dying—that is, dyeing the fabric she planned to sell. She was hunched over, stirring her cauldron, and the edges of her gray veil almost dipped into the steaming dye.

I ran to her, dodging the pointy shells lying in the dirt in front of her stand. The shells were the source of the rotting-fish smell, and the smell would get stronger as they basked in the afternoon sun. Our house was across the street, but the smell from the dyer's stand was offensive enough to keep anybody from wanting to be our neighbors.

The dyer handed me a knife, so I could extract slime from the shell to make her dye, but I shook my head. "Sorry, maybe later. Did you see a rider on a Nisean horse pass by?"

"A what?"

"A man riding a white horse."

She tapped her forehead several times. "I did see a man riding a horse."

"You did? Where did he go?"

"He turned left just past your house."

"Hmm." I looked over my shoulder. That was a dead end. "I wonder where he went?"

"He walked back up our street and went into your shop. Without the horse."

I thanked her, crossed the street, and rushed into the shop on the bottom floor of our house. The Persian stood in front of a display table with fishhooks, tent spikes, hammers, and chisels. He wore a white, long-sleeved shirt and baggy pants tucked into tall boots.

I didn't know the customary manner of greeting for Persians, so I was glad to be speaking to his back. "Peace be upon you. Have you seen the Behistun

Rock?" The Behistun Rock was said to be a huge rock in Persia, engraved with a life-sized relief of King Darius putting his foot on the chest of a prisoner lying on the ground. But the most exciting part was the mysterious inscriptions.

The Persian put down a spear, then turned around. "Peace be upon you. Yes, it is impossible to miss."

"So, it's not just a legend! Does it really give clues to the location of a secret treasure?"

"Locals say so," he said. "They refer to it as *Treasure Story*."

"Do you remember any of the clues?"

"No, I have no idea. Is the owner of the shop here?"

"You have never tried to decipher the clues?"

He laughed. "I have never wanted to scale a sheer cliff nearly 330 feet high."

That was 329 feet higher than I wanted to climb. I got dizzy just thinking about it.

"Behistun is not just a rock. It's a mountain." He shook his head, and the silver chain fastening his turban jingled. "You did not know?"

I felt like that prisoner with a boot on my chest. I had given up ax throwing and extracting slime to follow a lead that wasn't worth pursuing.

I didn't have time to cross Behistun Rock off my treasure map because I heard the sound of hammering coming from the courtyard behind the shop. Had I put the bag of limestone right where I was told? If I had forgotten to put it out, what kind of response would it garner? Yelling? For sure. Throwing something? Probably. Being called Slapdash?

Shem's booming voice breached the shop door. "Eli!" At least he referred to me by my name.

If Shem ever met Jesus, he would probably tell Him that He walked on water the wrong way. What kind of person does that? The man who was not only my uncle but also my master. By that, I mean that I was his metalsmithing apprentice.

I excused myself from the Persian and called out, "I'll be right there!"

Behind the shop, the u-shaped, stone walls of our house created a courtyard which Uncle Shem turned into his workshop. He didn't look up when I walked in, but I spotted the bag of limestone next to his anvil. What a relief! I had put the bag right where he had told me to put it.

He was pounding a piece of copper with a planishing hammer to smooth out the dents. "Eli, I need you to do this. Add that and stir."

This? That? Being able to interpret clues was a good skill for a treasure hunter, and I was getting a good deal of practice. Next to the limestone was a bag of manganese, a pile of ashes, and a bucket with some liquid. "Should I mix all three in there?"

He pointed to the limestone and the ashes. "No, just this and that. When it's a thick paste, put it there." He motioned to the wood table along the side wall.

"Yes, Uncle Shem." I moved the bucket closer to the limestone. "Oh, there's a customer in the shop, from Persia."

Uncle Shem hung the planishing hammer back on the wall in line with a row of hammers arranged from smallest to largest. He rushed into his shop, taking off his leather apron and putting on that wide smile he reserved for customers only.

I dumped the limestone and the ashes into the bucket, then grabbed a metal rod and began stirring. Long after my arm started to ache, the mixture still dripped instead of plopped, so I switched hands and stirred faster. The mixture was thickening but not yet to Uncle Shem's specifications. Granted, he wasn't the most specific person.

When I was done, I carried the bucket over to the table, and from there I could hear the Persian talking to Uncle Shem.

"I heard you make a mirror with a reflection that's better than looking into the sea."

"Well . . ." Uncle Shem paused a moment.

Two small mirrors were lying on the table in front of me, and these mirrors weren't the polished brass type that wealthy people had. The Lebanese had invented a new kind with perfectly clear reflections by pouring molten lead onto blown glass, and Uncle Shem had been trying to duplicate the process.

In the first mirror, my round face appeared as skinny as a camel's. In the second, my mouth stretched from my chin to my eyebrows. When I bowed my head, my eyes seemed to grow to the size of onions.

Uncle Shem cleared his throat. "How did you hear that?"

"I'm in a hurry, but I'd like to buy one."

"I'll have one ready soon. When do you need it?" Uncle Shem asked.

"Could I get it by the sixth hour?"

"Certainly."

Uncle Shem walked back into the courtyard and saw me looking at the failed mirrors. "I think I figured out how to fix that," he said.

I stood at attention.

"Yesterday, I was just Shem the metalsmith, but today I'll be Shem, the first Israelite to make this new kind of mirror."

"I can't wait to see it," I said.

He lifted a spoonful of my mixture, and it plopped back into the bucket. "We'll use that later. Good job getting everything ready."

Just like that, I stood a foot taller. Why did one compliment from him mean more than ten from Mama?

When he pulled a sheet of glass out of the furnace, I backed up to get out of the way but tripped on a pair of tongs leaning against the wall.

He rolled his eyes. "You're so clumsy you're going to fall off this flat earth someday."

I scrambled up, wiping the dirt off my tunic. It's terrible to admit, but I wasn't sure I wanted Uncle Shem to succeed in making the mirror.

He placed the glass on the table. "Now we pour the lead on."

"Want me to get it?" I asked, *trying* to be helpful.

"We'll both have to. It's heavy."

We walked over to the firepit, and Uncle Shem handed me a metalsmith apron. I inhaled the leather scent as I put it on. It must've weighed ten pounds, and the hem dragged along the ground. The leather was so stiff I could only walk half my normal stride.

He pointed to a bucket of molten lead hanging over the fire. "Grab the handle."

As soon as I wrapped my hand around the handle, my fingers recoiled as though I had touched the burning bush itself. It wasn't as hot as the molten lead, but it sure did hurt.

"Why don't you have gloves on?" he asked.

I put on gloves, and we staggered to the table with the bucket as waves of the sizzling liquid swished back and forth.

"You hold it. I'll pour," he said.

I held the glass straight up and down.

He scowled. "No, the other way."

I turned the glass facedown.

"This had better work." He carefully poured the lead onto the glass. "Now set it down in the tray."

We waited in silence while the lead hardened, and the tray formed the mirror's straight edges.

As Uncle Shem paced back and forth, I took off my gloves and cooled my burning palm and fingers on the leather apron. Finally, he lifted the glass out of the tray and turned it over. "Now you should start to see your reflection."

I waved the smoke away and we stared at the glass. Our hazy reflections started to become clear and soon they were crisp, unlike anything I had ever seen.

In fact, the smile on Uncle Shem's face was one I had never seen. He was looking at me with pride. My reflection looked surprised until I realized that his reflection wasn't looking at me. The pride was directed toward the mirror.

He let out a low whistle. "It's amazing."

"You really are going to be famous," I said.

"Now take it off," Uncle Shem commanded.

Did he mean the mirror or the apron? I was confused. "Do you mean—"

"Hurry up!" he yelled.

I grabbed the mirror, then everything went in slow motion. The edges were still searing. I rushed to set it back down but tripped on the apron. The gravel crunched as my feet slid out from under me.

I tried to take back what I had thought about not wanting him to succeed. I saw everything diagonally—the steaming bucket, Uncle Shem's boots, and an ember lying in the gravel. I silently screamed, *No, no, no, don't let it break!* The mirror and I crashed to the ground.

Time sped up. My stomach flinched, then rolled into a ball and played dead.

CHAPTER 2

THE TREASURE CHEST THAT CLEARS THE WAY

Dozens of mirror shards lay on the ground, reflecting dozens of angry Uncle Shems. The veins in his neck protruded like gnarly tree roots. His gloved hands covered his head as if he was keeping it from flying off. He threw the largest remaining piece of glass against the table.

My body went limp, but my throat got tighter and tighter. "I'm so sorry. I feel terrible. I didn't mean . . ." I started to get up, bending the stiff apron with my torso.

"You slapdash! You are just like your father."

15

His words pushed me back down. Why did he have to say that? I could handle being called names, but for him to make fun of the way Papa died . . .

He bent down close to my face. His pupils were elongated like viper eyes and his whisper was a growl. "Get out." The growl became a shout. "Get out!"

Did he mean get out of the courtyard or our home? I lifted off the apron and ran through the pine trees at the back of the courtyard.

I headed out of the village to a watchtower where I often went to think. Construction had stopped years ago, and half the wood had been scavenged, leaving two walls of the tower, part of a balcony, and a limestone foundation.

Weeds surrounded it except for the red roses Mama had planted on the spot where Papa died. He had been building the third story when one of the railings broke and he fell.

I sat on the bottom rung of a decrepit ladder leaning against a wall. The ladder teetered as I shakily exhaled. Would Uncle Shem ever be able to make another perfect mirror? The one I broke was worth a small fortune. Would I have to quit school and get a job to pay for it? Uncle Shem would probably like to sell me into slavery, which couldn't be that much worse than living with him.

Even if Uncle Shem forgave me, I could not spend my life working for him. A hotheaded metalsmith who can't give directions mixed with a clumsy slap-dash would turn a workshop into a crucible.

I stood up and stepped back so I could see the broken railing dangling from the balcony. Papa would've known what I should do. The weathered wood reminded me of the time Papa carved Noah's ark and inscribed something about patiently waiting for the rainbow. Another time he made a sling-shot with the words of King David, "Take courage and be a man." That encouragement plus more detailed instructions would've been helpful right then. I charged at the side of the ladder and pushed it to the ground. It landed in the weeds, framing them in perfect squares.

I stared down on the foundation where I had used a green malachite stone to draw a huge map of the world. I had put Xs on all the places I planned to look for treasure. Treasure hunting would be my way out of being Uncle Shem's apprentice. When I discovered a few one-of-a-kind treasures, everyone would agree that my skills would be put to better use finding ancient artifacts and lost cities.

I scribbled over Behistun Rock, then let my eyes glaze over, somewhere between the lost city of Atlantis in the middle of the sea and the Lighthouse of Alexandria. While the lighthouse didn't hold undiscovered treasure, it was something I had always wanted to see. I definitely didn't want to go up in the lighthouse. Why take a chance that the railing would hold? But I could imagine being on a ship at night, watching the massive firelight reflecting off the black waves.

Rain pelted me back to reality. Every winter the heavy rains washed the map away, forcing me to draw it over from memory. I had just drawn it again last week, thinking that the rainy season was over, but I was wrong. Raindrops turned the straight lines of the map into feathery streaks. Soon green streams of water swept across the drawing of the lighthouse and through the sea. Alexandria disappeared and finally Atlantis. I wasn't sure I'd ever draw it again.

I could not spend another day as Uncle Shem's apprentice. I had to find treasure right away. And

I had to find something really important. What was the most valuable treasure out there?

I studied what was left of the map for over an hour without any inspiration, and started to rest my head in my hands when I noticed the burns. On my right hand, the hot bucket handle had created red stripes across the top of my palm and the middle of my fingers. Because of the searing mirror, all my fingertips were bright red, and the skin was smooth, but there were no blisters.

I was fortunate, though not quite as fortunate as the three Israelites who emerged unharmed after the King of Babylon threw them into a fiery furnace. We referred to that as *The Irrefutably Providential Fire-Proofing Incident* because it was enough to prove the power of the one true God, even to a skeptical heathen king.

Of course, miracles like that weren't common in my village. The fire-proofing miracle happened five hundred years ago, after the Babylonians destroyed the old Temple in Jerusalem. At least the prophet Jeremiah had the foresight to get the Ark of the Covenant out of the Temple beforehand, hiding it in some remote cave. Since then, the Temple had been rebuilt but the Ark had never been found—the Ark of the Covenant! That was the ultimate lost treasure! God may not have let me emerge unscathed, but it seemed He was showing me a way out of the crucible.

The Ark was a large chest made of acacia wood and covered in pure gold with two golden angel statues on top. The Babylonians may have considered it nothing more than a valuable piece of art, but we Israelites knew it was far more than that. According to one source, as some Israelites carried the Ark, two flames shot out the bottom of the chest, burning snakes, scorpions, and thorns along the way. Another legend said that the Ark bearers didn't have to carry it. Instead, they were lifted off the ground and floated along beside it. In case that theory was wrong, I needed to find three brawny men to help me carry it.

Even more astounding was that the Ark gave people a chance to meet with God. Well, not all people, just one priest, one day a year. On the Day of Atonement, the priest could go into the Temple, behind the veil to the restricted area called the Holy of Holies, and speak to God who dwelled there above the Ark.

I imagined the men and me returning the Ark to the Temple. Cheering crowds parted like the Red Sea as we climbed the steps. The men in the crowd patted us on the back, praising our skills and courage.

Finding the Ark would solve everything. I took off toward the market, feeling more like a treasure hunter and less like Slapdash.

CHAPTER 3

ARK BEARER

My friend Abel would make a good Ark bearer, mainly because he would enjoy floating alongside it. In the time it took to walk from the tower to the market where Abel worked, I developed a reasonable plan to find the Ark. I stood about twenty feet away from his father's stand and waved Abel over.

He started walking toward me and sped up as he saw small patches of blood on my chest and rope belt. "Are you all right?"

"I just cut my finger on some glass in the court-yard," I said.

"Did Shem throw something? Or call you Slap-dash? Why do you let him get to you?" Abel asked.

"It's nothing. And I must keep the peace for my mother's sake."

He shook his head and did something highly unusual. He stopped talking. Normally even locusts couldn't get a sound in when Abel was around, so this was my chance to say it. Abel and I were best friends. In fact, I was his only friend, so why was my heart racing? I whispered and tried to sound spontaneous, "Why don't we try finding the Ark of the Covenant?"

He shielded the sun with his hand, so he could see if I was serious. Even the locusts remained motionless.

Usually Abel's thoughts spilled all over the place, but I needed to pull them out one by one and slay each objection. I began slowly. "Why not?"

Abel blinked rapidly. "Why not? Because I'd like to live to the age of thirteen!"

I was ready for that one, but it would be the most difficult to overcome. Who could forget that someone died just by touching the Ark? I gave a vague but confident rebuttal. "We'll be careful."

"I know you probably have the whole thing planned, or you wouldn't have brought it up, but it's been missing for hundreds of years," he said. "What makes you think we can find it?"

What a relief that Abel had quickly gotten over his desire to live! I kept moving the idea forward. "Precisely because we live right now."

"What do you mean?" he asked.

"One hundred years ago would've been too soon. One hundred years from now will be too late," I said.

Abel leaned toward me as if I were a dying man revealing the location of buried treasure.

I whispered, "The Son of God is present on the earth right now. Surely He knows where the Ark is."

Abel stared at the Galilean hills and slowly nodded. "Yes. Yes, of course, Jesus knows." He looked back at me. "But why would He tell us?"

"Jesus is not going to be with us forever. When He's gone, we're going to need God's Presence in the Temple."

Abel started snapping his fingers. "Couldn't Jesus just snap His fingers and return the Ark Himself?"

I had to think before I responded. The Messiah came to set captives free, even those of us who were captives in our own homes. I wasn't confident about much, but I was sure that Jesus would help if I could just explain my situation, although I couldn't say that.

Instead, I replied, "He's so busy raising dead people and curing the sick, He'll appreciate people wanting to help Him for a change."

Abel stopped snapping his fingers. "Well, let's try. And I promise to do more than hold the lantern this time."

Objections slayed! The locusts began humming.

"This will be better than discovering all the gold in King Philip's tomb. We've got to talk to Jesus before someone else does." Abel shook off his pessimism, but it splattered back on me.

I sighed. "That's the part that will take an act of God. Mama and I have been to Cana, Magdala, and Capernaum, but we keep missing Him."

"Maybe Jesus will pass through the village and stay at your mother's inn," he said. "So many pilgrims are already headed to Jerusalem."

First of all, what Abel called an inn was just one room that we rented out to travelers. Secondly, the odds were not in favor of Jesus coming to our boring village. I had a better chance of getting leprosy, but I never liked to correct poor Abel.

I looked over his shoulder and saw a man walking away from a different stand. He was carrying a lamb and didn't realize he was being chased by a woman waving a tent spike. "Somebody's causing trouble," I said.

"A Greek or Roman?" Abel asked, turning around.

The woman screamed in unison with the lamb's squeal. The lamb jumped out of the troublemaker's arms, and he turned around and watched it run back to her. The man's facial features were concealed by unkempt long hair and an even longer beard.

"Huh. Could be an Israelite," I said.

When the lamb reached the woman, she stopped running and dropped the tent stake. She threw some coins at the man. "Take it all back. You're not keeping Lamby." Then she spat at him with the precision of a camel.

"Wonder what he did?" I asked.

Abel began speculating on all the possibilities.

The man strode past all the stands, and it seemed he was about to leave town. Just after passing Uncle Shem's shop, he looked back and must've seen the curtain in front of our door, notifying pilgrims that we had a room available. He turned around and headed back. This was not the kind of pilgrim to welcome into our home.

Abel was still speculating. "Or maybe he's going to use the lamb for his Passover sacrifice, or maybe he's planning to feed it to the pack of wolves that raised him, or maybe . . ."

I took off running toward our house, yelling over my shoulder, "Sorry, Abel, I have to go!" I ran past all the stands and finally the dyer's table. My mind felt like that bubbling cauldron. I wasn't ready to face Uncle Shem. How would he react to my being back home? Had Mama found out that I broke the mirror and wasn't as capable as she thought? Was she welcoming the troublemaker?

CHAPTER 4

CONFRONTATION

I nstead of running through Uncle Shem's store, I sprinted up the outside steps that guests used to reach our living quarters on the second floor. Sure enough, when I opened the door, the troublemaker from the market was there, standing next to Mama.

"I'm so glad you're here, Eli." She smiled and introduced me to the man whose name was Timon. Wiry hair partly covered his wrinkled, sweaty forehead. It seemed that his beard might be home to a bird egg or two. And his grumpy face looked as though I had actually said that out loud.

After we greeted one another, she said, "Timon just started telling me about seeing Jesus. Timon, please sit down and kindly start from the beginning." She pulled out cushions for us, but I remained standing.

Timon uncrossed his arms, accidentally revealing a dagger under his shabby cloak. "A few days ago, I was walking in the hills when I saw Jesus speaking to a crowd. I listened for a bit and afterwards His followers passed out bread and fish to all the people. At first everyone was quiet, thinking about His words, but slowly people's voices got louder and louder. Women rushed from one group to the next. Men looked at the sky and shook their heads. Apparently, Jesus had taken five loaves of bread from a boy and turned them into thousands of loaves of bread."

"That's the sign!" I blurted out.

Timon raised his scarred eyebrow. "What do you mean?"

"He's the Messiah. It is said that the Messiah will give us miraculous bread from heaven, a new kind of manna," Mama explained.

"Huh." Timon smiled tentatively, then broadly. "Well, there you have it. I've heard that He'll be in Jerusalem for Passover, so I'm on my way to meet Him."

"Great beard of my father! That's amazing!" I exclaimed.

Mama clapped her hands. "Of course. Jerusalem at Passover! We're heading there tomorrow."

"We've been trying to meet Jesus for months but keep missing Him," I added.

"This time it seems certain," he said.

Treasure hunters live by possibilities, not certainties, but it seemed my plan was falling into place. We'd leave for Jerusalem tomorrow, meet Jesus, find the Ark, and try not to die while carrying it to the Temple.

Just then Uncle Shem came up the stairs, walked past me toward the kitchen table, and pretended he didn't see me.

Mama tried to bring him into the conversation. "Our guest was just with Jesus of Nazareth."

"Hmmmpf," Uncle Shem mumbled, then opened the cupboard and pretended he didn't see Timon.

She raised her chin as if to catapult her words over the cupboard door. "He's got proof that Jesus is the Messiah. He gave the people bread from heaven."

Uncle Shem snickered and looked Timon up and down. "You expect me to believe that a bandit has figured out the identity of the Messiah?"

Timon clenched his fists, then stood up so he could hold Uncle Shem's stare. "He's right. I was—I guess I always will be—a bandit. But I'm trying to change."

"You can't change who you are," Uncle Shem said.

Timon palmed the hilt of the dagger in his sheath and began stepping toward Uncle Shem. "You're trying real hard to make people think you've changed."

Mama's eyes grew wide.

"Have you? Or are you still foolish?" Timon asked.

Uncle Shem shifted from one foot to the other, then narrowed his eyes.

Mama could smooth things over better than a floured rolling pin. She turned to Timon. "We'd love to hear more about Jesus's talk, but you must be tired. Eli will show you to your room."

Timon and I didn't move.

Uncle Shem unlocked his gaze and turned to Mama, his gravelly voice full of the smoke and soot he'd been standing over all day. "If you're going to let him stay here, keep him away from my business."

Mama picked a piece of lint off her cushion and didn't look up.

Uncle Shem went down the steps. The thick air followed him like a galley slave.

"Please let us know if we can do anything to make you more comfortable," Mama said to Timon.

His squinty eyes darted around the room. "Actually, there is something you can do." He handed her his dagger. "Having it is always a temptation."

"I understand." Mama took it and handed it to me.

I was happy to rid the stranger of any temptation to harm the insulting innkeepers. The bottom of the hilt featured a sculptured eagle, but it had been worn down as if Timon scratched it on a rock to desecrate Rome's symbol of power.

Timon shrugged his shoulders and appraised his own appearance. "It's not easy to come by honorable employment."

"It's even harder to come by a Roman dagger," I said.

Mama glared at me. "Eli!"

It wasn't as much fun when she used her rolling pin on my observations.

Timon wasn't baited into explaining the dagger. He continued, "I'm trying to become a shepherd. Nobody trusts them either, but at least it's an honest living."

"And you'll be able to stay in the hills, which you probably enjoy," Mama said.

Timon nodded. "Well, thank you for your hospitality."

I put the dagger in a drawer. My shellfish knives looked puny next to it. I showed Timon to his room and raced back upstairs.

Mama was taking some coins from her basket of yarn. "I've been saving up. Now with the money Timon will pay us, we can rent a donkey and get to Jerusalem in four days instead of nine."

"But can we still leave tomorrow as planned?" I asked, rolling out my sleeping mat on the floor between the cushions and the kitchen table.

"Yes, but we'll travel in a different caravan than Abel. You and he won't be able to go exploring for glowworms."

"I'll just have Abel meet me at the olive groves on the tenth day of Nisan."

"Ah, at the lamb races. When I was young, I never wanted to bond with the lambs, knowing that in a few days they'd be sacrificed."

"Meeting up with all my friends at the lamb races is one of my favorite parts of the trip," I said.

"My favorite part is that moment when we're waiting in the middle court at the Temple while the men sacrifice our lambs, and the priests pour the blood on the altar. Two million Israelites singing and giving glory to God. It gives me chills every time."

And that would be the perfect moment to return the Ark to the Temple. I lay down on my mat. "I just hope we can find Jesus among two million people."

She blew out the candle on the table and began walking to her room. "Providence will guide us."

I knew Providence would guide us. Now if He would just schedule everything so Uncle Shem wouldn't be with us when we met Jesus. Though Uncle Shem always presented our lamb at the Temple and led the Passover meal rituals, he never participated in the festivities around Jerusalem. What was Timon implying about Uncle Shem's past? Did Mama know what he meant?

And shouldn't we be a little worried about a bandit sleeping downstairs? Sure, he gave me his dagger, but the shop was full of swords. I didn't want to prolong the day by trying to figure it all out. I was hoping to quickly fall asleep and put an end to my last night under Uncle Shem's roof. If we were still alive in the morning, I'd ask Timon to meet up with us in Jerusalem and help carry the Ark to the Temple.

CHAPTER 5

UN-ABLE TO MOVE

hen I awoke the next morning, the house was quiet. Normally Mama was awake and already saying her prayers. I peeked into her room, and she was lying on her mat.

Her cheeks were as white as the ceiling, and her voice was hoarse. "Eli, can you please pour me some water?"

"Mama, are you okay?"

"I think I just need to rest awhile."

I put a cup of water up to her chapped lips. After drinking she fell asleep, moaning occasionally, and I dabbed her face with a cool cloth.

I said my morning prayers plus some extra ones, asking God to heal her and help us leave for Jerusalem soon.

Then I prepared a basket of food for Timon, containing wildflower honey, black olives, plump red grapes, creamy goat cheese, and barley bread. I was so worried about Mama that even the smell of freshly baked bread didn't appeal to me.

I went downstairs and Timon opened the door before I could knock. His scowl contrasted his cheerful words. "Morning. Are you about ready to leave for Jerusalem?"

I handed him the basket. "No, my mother isn't feeling well, so we'll wait a bit longer. I should be getting back to her."

"Mind if I check on her? Living off the land has taught me a few things," he said.

Weren't bandits the ones that inflicted pain, not relieved it? But I wouldn't turn down anything that could help Mama. "I'd appreciate that."

Mama's room only had space for her on her mat, a stool, and Timon, so I waited outside.

When he walked out, I studied his face, hoping it would tell me there was no need to worry. His lips were clamped together as though he had sealed them with wax. He patted my shoulder with all the tenderness of a porcupine.

I recognized that gesture of pity and it sent prickling needles down my back.

Finally, he spoke. "Well, I can tell you're taking good care of her. What we need is some herbs. I'll go to the market."

I went back into Mama's room. Her breathing was heavy. I knew I should go tell Uncle Shem but didn't want to leave her alone.

Then there were long pauses between each breath. I stood up to go get help but couldn't move, couldn't even breathe myself until she finally exhaled.

Uncle Shem appeared in the doorway. "There better be a good reason the goat won't stop bleating."

I cleared my throat. "I'll milk her. Mama has a fever, and her breathing isn't right." I walked out of the room and watched him walk in.

He felt Mama's forehead, then rubbed his beard. Was he worried about Mama or about all the work not getting done?

"Timon went to the market to get herbs," I said.

Uncle Shem turned around. "I hope he doesn't meet that boy. What's his name? Abel, better known as *Un-Abel to Stop Talking*. Otherwise he won't return for weeks."

I tried to force a smile.

He hurried past me toward the stairs. "I'll get some hot water to make a broth."

Both men returned to Mama's room at the same time.

Timon handed Uncle Shem a bag that smelled like vinegar, oregano, and rotten cheese, then asked, "Would you like me to stay a few days and help out?"

Uncle Shem frowned. "We'll manage."

"Well, I hope you'll make it to Jerusalem," Timon said.

Uncle Shem replied with a sharp tone. "It's Passover. We're devout Israelites."

Timon stared at him, then picked up his bag. "Well then, I'll see you there."

I stepped forward. "Maybe I could go with you?"

Faster than a slamming door, both men's heads turned to look at me.

CHAPTER 6

FALLING, BUT NOT OFF THE EARTH

obody moved. I couldn't believe I had said it out loud. What was I thinking? Going to Jerusalem with a stranger, a bandit even? I had gotten caught up in the idea of getting out of this house. Of meeting Jesus. Perhaps I could get Him to come and heal Mama.

But that could take weeks, and if something happened to her while I was gone, I'd never forgive myself.

Timon looked at Uncle Shem. Uncle Shem looked at me.

My impulsiveness scurried away as it's prone to do. "Ah, never mind. We'll just see you there."

After Timon left, the days passed slowly. Good thing I stayed in Galilee because Uncle Shem didn't help care for Mama. His concern for her seemed sincere, but only to the extent that it didn't impact his business. Each day he ignored me, other than giving me lots of work on non-fragile items. I did all Mama's chores and mine. In between, I filled her pitcher, made her soup, and waited for her next breath. Though they were labored, they kept coming.

When Uncle Shem had to deliver a sword to a Greek customer, he asked me to watch the shop. I wasn't sure why I needed to watch the shop because there was practically no one left in the village. Every other Israelite had long since left for Jerusalem to celebrate Passover. The Temple there was the only place we could sacrifice Passover lambs, so Uncle Shem and I couldn't celebrate. As I sat at the counter, the sun streamed through the window, warming my aching back. I lay my head down on my arms and imagined what was going on in Jerusalem.

I fell asleep and when I awoke, it was dark already. How long had I slept?

The swords hanging from the ceiling started clanging, then the whole house shook. I covered my head and ducked under the stone counter. What was I supposed to do in an earthquake? Run outside? Stand in a doorway? Stay put? Glass fell from the countertop above me and crashed to the floor, commanding me to stay put.

But Mama was upstairs alone. On a good day, even idle stairs seemed like they were out to get me. Could I climb up the staircase as it was falling? I had to try. I ran to the steps, hoping the swaying swords couldn't reach me.

Being on the first step was like being blindfolded and standing up in a cart while crossing the rocky desert. I palmed the shuddering walls, but they were not supportive. Running didn't seem possible, so I decided to crawl. At least I would cut down on the distance I'd fall. With each step, my hands and knees landed on sharp pieces of plaster.

At the top, I sprinted over the rolling floor until I reached Mama's room, but my foot slid on her blanket and I fell backwards, banging my head on the stool.

When I woke up, I was lying on my mat and someone had put a cool towel on the top of my head. Papa? No, if it was Papa, then I was dreaming. I opened my eyes, but it was completely black. Did I go blind when I hit my head?

I heard approaching footsteps and listened for Mama's cracking ankles. As I sat up and reached for the bump on my head, my hand grazed the arm of whoever was helping me. The forearm was muscular but smooth. The arm hair had been singed off by fire—the arm of a metalsmith. Uncle Shem had taken care of me? Who would've thought?

"Go back to sleep. She's fine," he said.

The next time I woke up, it was light out. Light! I could see the light, then the cushions, the table, and the wall. Whoo! I didn't go blind! I thanked the Creator who protected us when creation did the unexpected.

My mat was sprinkled with dried blood and bits of plaster. I barely touched the knot on my head, and it throbbed. Though some dishes had fallen from the cupboards, the house had withstood the quaking. Papa had built it well.

I rushed into Mama's room, and she was sleeping. The floor was still damp, and a clay fragment from a broken pitcher lay next to her blanket, waiting to target bare feet. I picked up the shard and threw it out the window. Uncle Shem had brought her a new pitcher with fresh water.

Across the street at the market, Greek vendors picked up the wares that had been strewn on the ground. Canvas canopies that had once blocked the sun now blocked the road. The poor vintner turned his jugs upright, frowning at the ground that had its fill of red wine.

Some sheep ran through the leaning tents, leaving red-wine footprints behind them. The last sheep, an extra fluffy one, fell in a puddle of wine and its shriek sounded human. It emerged with a crimson belly. That was one way to dye the wool.

I raced to the shop, and Uncle Shem was crouched down, picking up broken glass.

"You all right?" he asked, barely looking up.

"Yes, you?"

"Fine. I was in the courtyard." He stood up and studied me as if my face would reveal the answer to his unspoken question. When I didn't respond, he said, "Remember?"

"I can't remember much," I said. What was he getting at? Did he know I fell asleep while watching the shop? "Thanks . . . thanks for helping me last night."

"Last night?" He finished the conversation by pointing out a fact the way you'd point an accusing finger. "You really hit your head."

I bent down and started picking up pieces of glass to preempt the next accusation, being called lazy. The compassionate Uncle Shem had been a phenomenon as short-lived as the earthquake.

CHAPTER 7

DELIVERANCE FROM DEATH

Besides Uncle Shem and Mama, who weren't speaking to me for very different reasons, the only people I saw were those I spotted out the window as I sat at Mama's bedside. Pilgrims began coming back from Jerusalem, but I was too busy to host guests, so I took down the curtain that welcomed them. Without that income, I had to dip into the money that we had planned to spend on a donkey just to reimburse Uncle Shem for my food. Since I couldn't go to synagogue school, each night I practiced my memory work, so my rabbi would be pleased.

One night I took warm, melted candle wax, molded it into the shape of the Temple, and left it on Mama's windowsill. Had someone found the Ark of the Covenant? Was Jesus still in Jerusalem? Each night I added another waxed building until I had created a replica of Jerusalem. The miniature Tower of Light was leaning, and the amphitheater was about to fall off into the yard when Mama woke up. Her eyes were no longer glassy, and her cheeks had a touch of crimson.

"Mama! How do you feel?"

"Much better. How long have I been ill?" she asked.

I estimated based on the number of waxed buildings on the windowsill. "About eight weeks. Since right before Passover."

She rubbed her forehead and closed her eyes. "Did you meet Jesus?"

"I didn't want to leave you."

She placed her trembling hand on mine. "Oh. I wish you had gone with Abel's family. Despite what you think, Shem would've taken good care of me."

"How can you be so sure?"

"Trust me. He knows better than anyone about the importance of family loyalty."

Hearing our voices, Uncle Shem poked his head in, and Mama thanked us for everything *we* had done to help her. She was herself again, always believing the best about people, so why correct her?

"Tell me what's been happening," she said.

Uncle Shem opened his mouth to say something. Had he told her that I broke the mirror before she got sick, or was he about to reveal that news?

I braced myself.

Instead, he exhaled and closed his mouth abruptly.

No one said a word and Mama looked at him, then me. "How's business?" she asked, demonstrating that her ability to use the rolling pin to flatten rising tension had recovered nicely.

Uncle Shem went into a long description of all the products he was making for customers.

That evening we held a Todah, the sacrificial meal to thank God for helping us through a difficult time. Uncle Shem served sweet red wine and warm bread, then recited the psalm:

FOR THOU HAST DELIVERED MY SOUL FROM DEATH, MY EYES FROM TEARS, MY FEET FROM STUMBLING;

I WALK BEFORE THE LORD IN THE
LAND OF THE LIVING.

Despite the wine warming my throat, I shivered. The words to the psalm echoed in my mind: *deliverance from death, tears, and stumbling.* Why did I have the strange feeling that this was not the end of our trials? There were more to come.

CHAPTER 8

RELUCTANT SEND-OFF

ou know when you're digging a hole and your shovel hits something unexpected? The sound of metal scraping metal prompts the mind to imagine all the glorious possibilities. My shovel was about to hit something, though the only sound I heard was Mama and Uncle Shem talking as I lay half asleep on my mat.

"This is my last option," he said.

She whispered, "He can do it."

His voice became louder. "That remains to be seen."

I sat up and stretched.

Mama let Uncle Shem know I was awake by giving me an especially loud greeting. "Good morning!"

"Good morning, Mother, Uncle Shem. What's going—"

Uncle Shem stood up and the chair legs screeched as they were pushed across the floor. "I need you to make a delivery to a customer in Jerusalem."

I jumped up and my body tingled. It must've been my treasure-hunting instincts coming out of hibernation. "Yes, Uncle Shem. How soon should I leave?"

"Now. The customer needs it in six days."

I ran to the cupboard and started pulling out food. "I just need to gather a few things. What am I going to deliver?"

"A mirror," he said.

I steadied myself against the cupboard and dropped the olives. They rolled around the room, eagerly reinforcing Uncle Shem's doubts.

His mouth said nothing, but his eyes told Mama, "See? I told you."

I kneeled down and gathered the ornery olives as fast as I could.

He sighed. "I'll get the mirror."

As soon as he left the room, I stood up and whispered to Mama, "Deliver a fragile masterpiece over 120 miles in six days?"

"With as many times as you've been to Jerusalem, you'll have no problem getting there on time," she said.

"But we're always part of a caravan. Can't he hire another merchant to go? Or maybe a pilgrim who's going that way?"

"You know he doesn't get along with the other merchants. And we can't trust just anybody with the mirror. Wait until you see it. It's stunning."

"I have to tell you . . ." There seemed to be an olive pit in my throat. "So was the last mirror before I . . ."

She walked over and put her hands on my shoulders. "Shem told me. That was an accident. You can do this." She stepped aside and poked her head deep into a cupboard to find Papa's old leather bag.

I removed Timon's dagger from the drawer and stood there a minute, running my fingernail over the initials T.L. carved on the thick end of the blade.

Mama's head emerged from the cupboard. "Don't forget—" She gasped when she saw me holding the dagger. "I wish I could believe you wouldn't need that."

"I probably won't. Just for cutting vines and things," I said.

She bit her lip and studied me. "Go around Jericho, what with Herod and John the Baptist and all."

I didn't respond. What was the likelihood that I'd make it all the way to Jericho anyway? I put the remaining supplies in the bag. "I have a waterskin, dried meat, multiple loaves of bread—"

"Blessed goodness!" She put her hand to her chest. "I just realized. Providence has given you this opportunity to meet Jesus."

I froze until her words sunk in. "Huh. He might still be in Jerusalem." This was my chance. I had to meet Jesus. No matter what. "I'll find Him as soon as I deliver the mirror."

"That's my boy!"

After she wobbled to her room, I mumbled, "And if I don't deliver the mirror intact and on time, Jesus can raise me from the dead after Uncle Shem shatters me into little pieces."

She came back with a lantern, and Uncle Shem returned with the small mirror wrapped in wool and flanked by pieces of wood. He started to place it in my bag but stopped. "You need to realize it's worth three months' wages."

I tried to smile. "So, if I get even the tiniest scratch on it, I better not even bother coming home, right?"

He didn't smile. "Not only that, but if you arrive late, the customer will have already left town, and no one else will want it because it's personalized just for him."

I nodded with forced conviction. "I'll take good care of the mirror. You take good care of Mama."

"Here are instructions to find the customer," he said, handing me a scroll. Then he gave me his blessing.

Mama hugged me. "We'll see you in a couple weeks. May the angels lead you."

Somehow when I put my heavy traveling bag over my shoulder, I felt lighter than ever.

CHAPTER 9

UN-ABEL TO TALK

s I walked past the market, I thought everything was normal. After the earthquake, every merchant had put up a new canopy over his stand, forming a giant coat of many colors. Apparently, the earthquake had benefited the tentmakers.

I considered stopping to tell Abel goodbye but couldn't spare the time. I was almost at the last stand when he yelled the shortest sentence he was capable of.

"Eli!"

I turned around but didn't go back.

He shouted, "How's your mother?"

"Better, thank you. Sorry, I can't talk. I have to make a delivery in Jerusalem."

"You didn't hear what happened there?" he asked.

I rushed back and whispered, "The Ark?" I studied his face. A moment ago, it was rosy due to the light filtering through the red canopy, but it suddenly lost all color.

He sighed. "No, no. How do I say this? Remember long ago the prophets—"

His father yelled from the back of the tent, "Abel, come here!"

"Coming, Father." He glanced at his father, then started walking backwards and holding up both forefingers. "I can't believe you haven't heard. Just wait. You must hear this."

Across the street, some women were up on their rooftop terraces, rushing past the wet tunics on the clotheslines. At this end of town, the houses were connected, and the women lifted their dresses up to their ankles, so they could run from one side of the terrace to the other, sharing the day's news with the neighbors on each side. If only I got my news from them.

I watched Abel and his father try to coax three reluctant sheep out of their pen. The other sheep knew just how to obstruct them by taking turns blocking the gate. What a time for sheep to become intelligent! I started pacing, then finally walked back toward the pen.

"Sorry, I'm almost done," Abel said.

"I really have to go. My uncle . . ."

"Just a bit longer!" Right then, two sheep charged out of the gate headlong into a tent pole. Abel couldn't stop them, and the tent billowed down on him. Poor Abel. His lanky body became the tent pole, holding up the slanting side. Fortunately, there were plenty of people around to help him.

I strode away, calling over my shoulder, "I'll catch up with you as soon as I get back."

How could I have known that my impatience with Abel would result in more difficulties in Jerusalem? Waiting a few minutes longer to hear his news would've changed everything. I could have avoided my mortal enemy, but perhaps I wouldn't have found the treasure.

CHAPTER 10

THREATS

I tried to avoid eye contact. Still the merchant in the last stand yelled at me. "Hey, boy! I can see you need him." He patted the donkey right between its pointy ears. "Just two shekels a day."

I needed to travel twenty miles a day, and that overpriced donkey could walk more than forty, but I didn't have even one shekel to negotiate with. I shook my head and kept going.

My eye twitched each time the mirror bounced in my bag. I took a shortcut through the pasture of an abandoned farm, and there were ostrich feathers all over the ground. I picked one up and brushed my fingers along the vane. It was the softest thing I had ever felt and would make perfect padding for the mirror. I picked up about a dozen large feathers and placed them between the cloth and the pieces of wood, then gently tied a cord around it all.

I walked down a hill leading to the Sea of Galilee. Yellow flowers on the hill looked like Trojan soldiers marching down to meet the Greeks. They stopped when they reached the shore, but I marched on.

The sun started to set, so I forged a path through some weeds, stomping my feet to scare away snakes. A ridge near the top of a hill would block the wind, but that would mean I'd have to be up high. Instead, I set up camp at the base of the hill. It would be safer to have the mirror separate from my bag, so I hid it under some ferns.

Then I found some small rocks and placed them on the dusty ground to encircle a fire. I took flint out of my bag, but didn't want to use any of my meager supply of tinder yet. Beneath the ferns was a vacant bird's nest which would be perfect tinder. Once the fire started crackling, I leaned against a rock and let the heat warm my feet. Although I hadn't met my goal of walking twenty miles, it was a satisfactory first day.

I pulled out the tin cup Mama had given me for my twelfth birthday, filled it up with water, and placed it on a rock next to the growing flames. When the water began boiling, I emptied my bag of dried lentils, peas, beans, and cumin into the cup and stirred it with my gourd spoon.

Suddenly, something rustled in the woods. The fire was supposed to ward off predatory animals, but perhaps the smell attracted human predators. Nearly twenty-five feet beyond the low ferns was a dense forest that hid whatever was navigating toward the smoke.

My bag was on the ground out of arm's reach. I stretched my leg, but it wasn't long enough, so I reclined a bit more. My toe could touch it but couldn't snag the strap. Finally, my toe grasped it and I dragged the bag toward me. I just had time to put the strap over my head, so that I wore it diagonally across my body when two men emerged from the trees.

"You're not welcome here. Pay the mountain toll and move on," one of them said. He was stocky with tanned skin and a shaggy beard, and the other had a narrow head with little blond hairs standing up straight like spikes on a stalk of wheat. Without knowing their names, I thought of them as Stocky and Wheatie.

I jumped up. My mind raced through a thousand scenarios of how I should respond. Should I run? Even if I could outrun them, the mirror was still hidden in the ferns. Could I sneak back later and find it? If they caught me then, how would they react to finding me in their territory twice? What if they found the mirror before I could get back to it?

Wheatie fiddled with the rope dangling off his belt. "Yes, pay the toll. What do you have for us in your bag? Hand it over."

I didn't speak or move.

Wheatie's braided beard moved up and down as he spoke. "Can't you talk?"

"Of course I can." I was just too busy figuring out the odds of my skull ending up in those ferns or in a bone box like everybody else. Traditionally, after a dead body decayed in the family tomb, the bones were moved into a stone box to make room for the next victim. Each bone box was a little taller than a skull and slightly longer than a man's thigh bone. I pictured Mama cradling my empty bone box, then throwing it down in futility, knowing that my bones were lying somewhere between Galilee and Judea.

Stocky glanced at my leather bag and sandals. "Do you speak Greek as well as Aramaic?"

"Yes," I said, temporarily reassured because corpses didn't need to speak Greek or Aramaic.

"Can you read and write?"

"Yes." If only I hadn't worked so hard to please my rabbi.

Wheatie looked at Stocky. "What do you need him for? I can speak Aramaic and read a few hieroglyphs."

Stocky rolled his eyes. "A slave that can speak Aramaic and Greek might earn forty shekels when that caravan comes back through next week."

Should I have felt good that my life was worth more than twenty rented donkeys? Instead my throat tightened at the thought of being taken to a strange land and having to work in a quarry or on a galley. They'd feed me rotten food or worse, the kind that's unlawful for Israelites to eat.

"Ah. Good thinking. In the meantime, he can be my slave." Wheatie clapped his hands twice and said in a singsong voice, "Slave boy, get me something to eat. What delights do you have in your bag?"

If only I had more skills to defend myself. One time a Greek merchant tried to teach me how to box, but I was too clumsy.

"I don't have much in here, just some olives," I said. Then it occurred to me. Why not put my clumsiness to good use? I offered Wheatie a handful of olives, but before he could take any, I dropped them. The olives rolled on the ground and spread out like spiders running out of a nest. "Ooh, sorry."

Wheatie mumbled something about how a good slave shouldn't be so careless, and rushed to my side to pick them up. While he crouched down, balancing on his toes, I pushed him forward then stomped on his back, pinning him down and placing his surprised face inches from the fire.

I shifted all my weight to the leg standing on his back but knew I couldn't keep him down long, so I reached into my bag, grabbed Timon's dagger, and brandished it.

Stocky had started to grab a dagger out of his boot but stopped. He stared at the disfigured metal eagle on the dagger, shining in the remaining moments of sunlight. "How did you get that dagger?"

Wheatie twisted his neck to see. "You killed Timon?"

The idea was laughable but not under my circumstances. "You know Timon?" I asked.

Stocky's stance relaxed. "We haven't seen him in months."

"I'll give you information about him, but in exchange you have to leave me alone," I said.

Wheatie started to protest, but Stocky waved his hand, silencing him. "Fine."

I tried to keep my voice steady as my leg started to shake. "Can I get your word?"

Stocky smirked. "I give my word all the time. I keep it slightly less often."

I spoke quickly. "Timon stayed with us about two months ago. He's trying to become a shepherd. He gave me his dagger."

Wheatie lifted his head, and his beard dusted the dirt. "Timon just gave you his prized dagger? That doesn't sound like something he'd do."

Stocky's eyes glazed over as if he was remembering something. "Well, well. Old Timon. Quick to give away others' secrets but closely guards his own. If you gave him hospitality, we'll return the favor. You'll be fine here the rest of the night. On the south side of the hill, there's a spring to fill your waterskin."

I lifted my foot off Wheatie, who picked up the remaining olives and dusted them off.

I put the dagger back in my bag. "So, how did Timon get a dagger from a Roman?"

"He took revenge on a soldier who killed his sister's lamb," Stocky said.

I scowled. "Romans!"

As the pair turned to go, I heard Wheatie muttering, "Why would Timon lower himself to herding sheep? Imagine spending your life wandering around with noisy, half-witted creatures."

Stocky sighed and shook his head as if he knew all too well what that was like.

After the bandits went back into the forest, I sat down and exhaled. Though I wasn't hungry, I guzzled my soup. I put the mirror back in the bag and slept with the strap around my arm. Whoever said the forest is a quiet place has never tried to sleep out in it. I woke up at every sound and tried to analyze if it was a threat, a falling acorn, or a harmless critter.

The next morning, I filled my waterskin at the spring and set out early. I looked back at the hillside, expecting to see Wheatie and his granular hair waving at me, making sure I left. If I'd had any other dagger besides Timon's, that would've ended very differently. What were the chances that Timon was well-known among all the other bandits guarding the roads to Jerusalem?

CHAPTER 11

MISCALCULATION

The next two days of travel went well, but despite my growing distance from Uncle Shem, I could never completely get away from him. Granted, I could whistle, and no one complained. I could decide whether to sleep in an olive grove or an apple orchard. And I could create new lists.

I had so many mental lists. Each one was written on a scroll, rolled up, and tied with sinew from a deer. Why sinew from a deer? Since it was all imaginary, it could've been anything, but that's just how I imagined it. The scrolls stood up vertically in a treasure chest in my mind, so I could reach them when I had something new to add.

The newest one listed my favorite mountains. Mount Gilboa's peaks appeared to be snow-covered when the clouds rested on them, but the Judean mountains were powerful enough to speed up time. At least on Sabbath. Sabbath starts at sunset, but since the mountains blocked the setting sun, I had to start my Sabbath rest a little sooner just to be safe. It was a guilt-free break since Israelites were forbidden to work or travel on Sabbath, and the command came from an authority even higher than Uncle Shem.

Up ahead was a cave that I hoped was abandoned and I sped up to reach it. I had averaged twenty miles each day and expected to arrive in Jerusalem in three days . . . until something occurred to me. My whistle stopped mid-note and my legs stopped mid-stride. When I had started this journey and calculated how many miles I needed to walk per day, I had forgotten to account for not being able to travel on Sabbath. I forced my foggy brain to think through the calculations, each time reaching a conclusion that made my scalp sweat. To make up for the lost day, I would need to walk thirty miles each of the last two days.

I dropped down on the side of the road and looked at the vast area of land that lay before me. I removed a pebble stuck between my toes and considered how I could possibly walk ten extra miles a day. Surely Uncle Shem had calculated the distance ahead of time and knew I couldn't break Sabbath. Had he set me up for failure? No, he didn't want me to fail. He just didn't care what his success cost me. How is it that Uncle Shem could follow all of Israel's precepts so carefully, but could care less about the suffering of others?

What if I did break Sabbath just once? If I could continue walking at my aggressive, but manageable pace, I would certainly deliver the mirror on time, meeting the expectations of Uncle Shem and his customer. It would only be one time that I'd break the commandment. Other Israelites worked every Sabbath, not wanting to miss out on the business of Roman and Greek customers. I wasn't as bad as them. "It's just one time," I said aloud as if someone might agree with me.

Why was it so easy for some people to break the Sabbath commandment when they tried so hard to keep the other nine? Maybe because it didn't hurt anyone. That thought was like a gentle pat on my agitated conscience.

I lifted the bag over my head and set it down behind me. I had to figure out God's will without Uncle Shem's expectations hanging over my shoulders. Even wool and ostrich feathers couldn't stop them from getting to me.

But God had His own way of signaling me, and it wasn't a beautiful rainbow. A dark cloud appeared on the horizon, and this cloud buzzed. It was a swarm of locusts.

I grabbed my bag and ran into the cave. If the mountain blocked the sun, the locusts blocked the mountain.

They just kept coming like the locusts that devoured every plant in Egypt when the Pharaoh refused to let our people go. After God led the people out of Egypt, He made a covenant with them and explained that the holy day of rest symbolized the covenant. In fact, God had even commanded that anyone who worked on Sabbath must be killed. In our village, when the Sabbath-breaking merchants were threatened with stoning, they either quickly repented or moved to heathen nations. Since I was in an isolated area, I was safe from accusing eyes.

I shook my head and my wild-haired shadow mimicked me. I couldn't go my own way, then expect God to protect me. Breaking Sabbath offended God and hurt my soul. I vowed to obey God and trust Him to get me to Jerusalem on time. The rest of the journey would be grueling. There'd be an increased risk of not delivering the mirror on time—boy would my uncle be angry—and of missing Jesus, but it was the right thing to do.

The locusts passed over without landing, except for one that dropped to its death nearby. I bent down to examine its spiky legs that seemed to have elbows instead of knees. Or were the legs just put on backwards? Since touching a dead critter would make me unclean according to the law, I scooped it up with my gourd spoon and placed it in my bag. Its only purpose would be to remind me to be obedient.

I sat inside the cave and forced some dried meat down my parched throat. I tried to sleep, but the cave air was stuffy, so I found a spot outside where the breeze could play tag with me all night long. My cloak thrown on some moss made a comfortable spot for my head, and I fell asleep right away.

After saying my prayers the next morning, I decided to explore the cave and grabbed my lantern and bag. Searching for the Ark would be considered work, but if I happened to stumble upon it, that would be Providence's way of rewarding my obedience.

At the back of the cave was a narrow tunnel. I went in and blindly followed the sound of dripping water for some distance. Finally, light began to enter as the tunnel opened into a cavern. Boulders supported by rocky arches formed a tall, domed ceiling. A large opening in the middle of the ceiling allowed the sun to shine in, warming the pond beneath it. I blew out my lantern, left my tunic on a rock, and stepped into the pond, disturbing millions of sparkling mica flakes suspended in the water.

I dove down and swam for a bit, then floated on my back and felt the slippery mineral water enter my ears, blocking all sound except the gurgling of small waves. As I drifted, I watched the blue sky give way to the rocky ceiling.

Then I climbed to the top of a boulder that had a steady stream of water cascading down the forty-foot sloping side. I wasn't afraid to be up that high because if I fell, I'd land in the water. I sat down, then pushed off with my hands and slid down the rock, gaining momentum as I reached the steep grade. Water droplets sprayed my face, so I couldn't see anything as my body lifted off the rock and glided through the air. Finally, my tailbone landed with a thud, stinging as it scraped along the remaining few feet.

I raced to the top to slide again, then leaned back to make myself go even faster. After completing my thirteenth and fastest run, I thrust my arms up victoriously and sat there a moment. My reflection in the water reminded me of the mirror. I groaned at the thought of how far I had to walk the next day. What if I didn't make it in time? There was nothing I could do about it on Sabbath, so I ran back up and continued sliding.

At the other side of the pond, two boulders jutted toward each other, not quite touching. A stream poured over each boulder and the two came together to form a narrow, but powerful waterfall. I sat under it, letting the water massage my shoulders and back.

Then I sprawled out on a rock and took a nap. When I awoke, the dim light overhead meant that the sun was starting to set. I grabbed my belongings and walked toward the tunnel. Back in the outer cave, I devoured some fig cakes, dates, cheese, and bread. After I swallowed the last bite, three stars appeared, signaling the end of Sabbath and the end of my fun.

CHAPTER 12

RECKLESS

I had journeyed twenty-eight miles through the Jordan Valley, and wouldn't have guessed that I'd soon learn to overlook outward appearances to discover inner beauty. Before you get the wrong idea, remember that first and foremost, I was a treasure hunter.

Although I walked beside the river, it was saltwater and there was nothing to quench my thirst. Each time I blinked, my dry eyelids reluctantly peeled apart.

The next morning, I made good progress for the first two hours until the temperature dropped and thunder rumbled. The dark clouds, which weren't locusts this time, released a different plague. Hail began pelting me. I cradled my bag and hunched over to protect it. Due to the frequent flooding of the Jordan River, few people lived in that area and the sparse land didn't offer much shelter. Finally, I spotted another cave and sprinted towards it.

Once inside, I began pacing. Something didn't seem right about this cave. Almost as soon as the strange feeling came over me, I noticed, at the back of the cave, a bowl of shredded dandelions. My feeling grew into a realization right when I heard scurrying and the clanging of a bell behind me. I cautiously turned around, ready to plead pardoning for so rudely intruding upon the homeowner.

A leprous girl stood right in front of me. She gasped and spilled her jug of rainwater. "Unclean, unclean!" Just a few patches of white hair remained on her head and part of her nose was missing. She tightened her tattered cloak but couldn't cover the sores all over her arms and legs.

Without thinking, I waved her into the cave. "Come in. Sorry, I didn't know anyone lived here."

She looked around, but there was nowhere else to go. When lightning lit up the entire sky, the skin on her forehead, above where her eyebrows used to be, wrinkled in fear.

"Hurry!" I looked at the sky, afraid that if I glanced at her, she'd see my apprehension. I forced a smile and moved to the side, so the contagious girl had plenty of room to get past me to the back of the cave. "Would it be okay if I just stay here until it stops?"

She ran past me and whispered, "Yes."

How had she gotten leprosy? Had she taken care of an infected loved one, or had she been careless? Would I end up like her because of a moment of recklessness? I wiped my hands on my cloak despite knowing that the disease didn't spread by being exposed to a leper's touch but by her cough or sneeze. She was breaking the law, and I was now unclean according to the law.

I pretended to study the lightning bolts, then let out a long, casual whistle. "This is a bad one." Despite warning myself to get out of there before she sneezed, I continued talking. "I'm going to Jerusalem to meet the Messiah."

"Jesus of Nazareth," she said.

How did she keep up on happenings in the world?

Her sunken eyes sparkled. "An elderly woman from Jericho moved here with me—it's hard to keep track, but I think it was sometime back in Shevat—and when she saw how quickly the disease ravaged my body, she hid her condition and went in search of Jesus. She's going to plead with Him to come here and heal us."

"I'm sure He'll come soon." I wanted to reassure her, but what did I know about Jesus's comings and goings?

She tied her cloak around her face so that it covered her nose and mouth. Her words became muffled. "I met Him once."

It was my turn to gasp. "What's He like?"

"I don't know how to describe the feeling you get when you're with Him. It's like . . . it's like when I was little, and our family got lost on our walk home after Passover. My father carried me on his back because we were all tired and worried. I fell asleep and when I woke up, we were already home." Her white forehead turned red. "That probably sounds silly."

I shook my head. "No, I understand what you mean. He's powerful and trustworthy. Aren't we lucky that we live in Israel right now? Think of the prophets who longed for the Messiah but lived centuries too soon. Or if we had been born a hundred or a thousand years from now, Jesus would no longer be on the earth."

"Or if we had been born in Gaul or Persia, we might never even hear of Jesus," she said. "My father is Greek—I was an outcast even before I was a leper—but Jesus came to our home."

"You had Jesus all to yourself?" I asked.

"My five siblings kept interrupting each other to get His attention, but somehow He gave each of us His full attention. He has these kind eyes and a sincere smile that says, 'Tamar'—that's my name—'Tamar, I know you and I value you.' "

All along I had imagined Jesus as this legend or hero, someone I would admire from the back of a crowd and maybe get to speak to for a moment but never get to know. Imagine spending time with Him. Suddenly getting to know Jesus became the most important part of my mission. Even if He wouldn't tell me the location of the Ark.

Outside the hail was still falling, then jumping back up as though the ground was too hot.

Tamar continued, "After that, when the villagers threw rocks at us, I just imagined Jesus smiling at me."

She paused, but when she spoke again, I could hear her grin. "Then I ran."

I laughed. "Well, at least there are no mean villagers here." The solitary place was only good for hiding lepers and bandits. Then it occurred to me that it was exactly the kind of place to hide something valuable like the Ark of the Covenant.

I took my lantern and walked to the back of the cave, staying a safe distance of ten cubits from Tamar. "Have you ever explored back here?"

"No, that's where the scorpions and spiders come from."

I ran my hand along two stones stacked in front of an opening in the back wall. "Aren't you curious about what's behind this?"

She stepped back. "Small spaces make me nervous. I even feel claustrophobic in the fog."

I peered into the crack between the stones and saw a dim glow. Temple priests had reported that when God spoke from above the Ark, they saw a glowing cloud. Could it be?

I pushed the top stone as hard as I could, and it fell to the floor. Then I climbed onto the bottom stone and crawled until my head and shoulders entered the musty cave. Something wet brushed the back of my neck. In the second it took to turn my head around and see what it was, I imagined the worst—a netted trap, a cobra's tail, or a rat's nose.

Turns out it was a trap!

CHAPTER 13

UNEXPECTED SPECTACLE

Dangling above me were sticky threads hung by glowworms to catch prey. These traps were harmless to humans but not to flying insects. There must have been hundreds of strands hanging like bluish-green lightning bolts. The wall above the opening was covered with glowworms, each the size of my thumb and shining like a candle inside a robin's egg.

My voice echoed off the cave walls. "Great beard of my father! You won't believe what's in here!"

"Scorpions and spiders?" she asked.

"Glowworms!" I swiped the strands like they were strings on a harp, then watched them flutter.

"What are glowworms?" she asked.

"Come and see."

Her voice became quiet. "Don't want to."

"Only the opening is small. There's a lot of room inside," I said.

"I don't want to mess up my hair. It took months to get it like this," she joked.

I pretended not to hear. I always laughed at Abel's jokes, which weren't even funny, but should you laugh at someone making fun of herself?

I climbed back out. As soon as she saw me, her eyes widened. My tunic was embroidered with spider webs. "If I can move the bottom stone, you'll be able to walk inside instead of crawling through the opening."

"It looks awfully heavy," she said.

I quickly dug a hole to the left of the stone. I wedged my dagger underneath the right side, then put a small rock under the hilt. I pushed the stone as hard as I could. At first, it wouldn't budge, but finally it moved, first a little, then a lot. With one final heave, the stone fell into the hole, making a large opening for Tamar.

She put her hands on her hips. "What did I tell you? Easy."

I laughed, then went back in. "These are unbelievable."

Tamar poked her head in. "I've never seen anything so beautiful." She moved closer but remained at the entrance.

I sat down on the floor and stared up at the ceiling. The glowworms squirmed, and their slow movements created different designs on the wall—a slingshot, a horse, an angel. "The vaulted wall changes my depth perception, making the worms seem like distant planets."

"You're right. It's like a scene from a play in which a treasure hunter carried a bowl of turquoise gems but tripped, sending them flying into the air. Then those fickle Greek gods hung the gems in the sky." She quickly added, "Of course, the stories about the Greek gods aren't true."

I muttered, "But the part about a clumsy treasure hunter is plausible."

"I love how the Greeks always explain natural wonders in an amusing way," she said.

"These are definitely natural wonders. When they're hungry, they glow even brighter." I touched one of the squishy worms, and it wrapped around my finger. "This amazing creature is soon going to change into a gnat. It has no say in the matter."

She sighed. "Few of us get to choose our future."

"Very true." The glowworms changed designs again, this time forming the shape of an angry person behind the prison bar strands. I stood up, remembering that I was losing valuable time.

I tried to memorize the scene of thousands of glowworms shining brightly in case I never got to see them again. I grabbed the lantern and quickly examined the rest of the cave. The Ark wasn't there. "I've got to continue on."

"Maybe the storm's passed," she said, walking out.

I picked up my bag and counted to ten before following her.

We stood outside the cave, squinting in the sunlight.

"Look!" She pointed to my arm. "One came with you."

I pulled off a clinging glowworm and placed it on the wall. "In broad daylight, it's nothing special. Just a bald caterpillar."

"You went to a great deal of trouble so I could see the grand spectacle," she said. "Thanks to you, I won't be lonely anymore."

I started walking back into the cave. "If I find Jesus before your friend does, I'll bring Him to you." I took out all the food from my bag and placed it in her bowl, being careful not to touch any part of the bowl. Barley bread and dried meat would taste much better than bitter dandelions. "A little something in return for your hospitality."

She ran past me, pulled down the cloak that had been covering her mouth, and tore off a large piece of bread with her remaining teeth.

I enjoyed something better, the taste of my first success as a treasure hunter. It was time to start a new list, one with all the treasures I had actually found. In my mind, I created a long list and wrote *glowworms* at the top in green. Too bad no one else would risk walking into a leper's cave to see them. I had been extremely careful but still had to be examined by a priest. If I showed symptoms, or even if I didn't but the priest was overzealous, he'd cast me out of our village. On second thought, it would be less risky to find Jesus and let Him affirm that I was clean.

So much depended on my finding Jesus. If hail had forced me into a cave with glowworms, Providence was surely guiding me. Somewhere up there, He had melted the hail into warm raindrops, and I lifted my chin so they sprinkled my face as I strode on.

CHAPTER 14

GREEN AND GLISTENING

f I were a glowworm, I would've been shining like the sun. I was starving. My stomach yelled at me for giving all my food to Tamar.

With every step, my feet slid sideways on the slippery ground and mud oozed up between my toes. I wore the bag in front of me like a yoke so that if I fell sideways, I wouldn't land on the mirror, but the weight of my bag pulled on my neck. The effort of trying to stay upright while being food-deprived made me dizzy.

After two hours, I reached a dry road, and although it was made of sharp rocks, I made better progress. When I reached the shore of the Jordan River, I left my sandals and walked knee-deep into the water, hoping to clean the hardened mud from the hem of my tunic.

Nearby, the water flowed over a large stone and created a little waterfall as the elevation dropped about a foot. I lay facedown on a flat rock, letting my feet hang over the edge under the waterfall. I pressed my cheek to the cold slab and would've fallen asleep, except that I knew the time had come. The time to eat the locust. Perhaps it would give me the energy to walk all night and arrive in Jerusalem in the morning.

I had eaten locusts before, but usually they were fried in flour and drizzled with honey. The question was where to start on a raw one. I didn't want antennae tickling the roof of my mouth. The wings were a choking hazard. Perhaps I should start with the legs because I could swallow them without chewing.

I stepped down from the rock, and something green glistened in the water. It was wedged between the rocks, so I reached into the crevice, but it wouldn't budge. I dried my hand on my tunic and tried again. Finally, it moved and I pulled out a shimmering emerald. I rubbed its smooth surface and admired how it had been cut and polished. Perhaps it had belonged to an Egyptian pharaoh or a Persian king. It was another rare item to add to my *found treasures* list, but unlike the glowworms, I could keep this one—unless . . .

The dull gray mountain peaks indicated that Jericho wasn't far off. At sunrise, I could go there and trade the gem for a donkey, allowing me to easily arrive in Jerusalem on time. That would give me a chance to sleep a couple of hours, then catch a fish for breakfast. I wouldn't have to walk all night, and I wouldn't have to eat the locust. I thanked God for His provision.

I set the gem on a rock and dried off in the rushes, most of which were even taller than I was. I unrolled the goatskin scroll on which Uncle Shem had written directions, placed the gem in the middle, and rolled it back up. In each end of the scroll, I jammed a rock to keep the gem from falling out.

After pulling up some stalks for a cushion, I lay down. The noise of swooshing rushes stifled the memory of Mama's warning to go around Jericho to avoid Herod, and I fell asleep. Then I heard a thundering sound. Was it real or was it in my dream? The noise became louder and louder. I figured out what it was. It definitely wasn't a falling acorn.

CHAPTER 15

RISKY INVITATION

In the midst of the tall rushes, I sat up on my elbows as a horse galloped toward me. Its rider was looking back at another horse behind him. My sheep-colored tunic blended in with the rushes, so even if the rider had been looking ahead, he'd never spot me. But in two seconds, the horse's hooves would find me.

"Look out!" I shouted, rolling into the cold water. My hip and elbow dug into the stones of the riverbed, but my head awaited the serious pain.

I heard the horse lurching away, then hooves slowing down. I cautiously lifted my head from the shallow water.

The horse had turned around but was slowly circling back toward me. The rider jumped off. "Are you okay? I didn't see you there."

I stammered, "Yes, I'm fine."

The other boy dismounted and sprinted to me. "Jacob, you almost trampled him!"

"It was impossible for him to see me," I said. As I sat there stunned, I could feel myself being studied from head to toe.

The older boy held his gaze upon the bottom of my feet and winced.

I hadn't wanted to complain, but my feet were really shredded from walking on the sharp rocks. I stood up as fast as I could.

Jacob handed me a wool blanket from his saddlebag. "It smells like horse, but it'll help. I'm really sorry."

I wrung out the end of my tunic and started to dry off with the scratchy blanket. "Don't worry. It was nothing."

"Oh, it will be when I tell it. In fact, when I'm Jacob of Jericho, the Greatest Charioteer in the World, you'll want to tell everybody how I expertly maintained control and just missed your skull."

The horse and I were still shaking, but Jacob of Jericho was already joking about it. A breeze made my tunic cling to my back and I sneezed.

"We can't let you sleep out here," the older boy said. "Come home with us for the night, and we'll give you some dry clothes and food."

Food! Without antennae and eyes. "You live nearby?"

"You know that imposing, lavish palace in Jericho?" Jacob asked, apparently referring to King Herod's winter home.

Were these Herod's sons?

Jacob smiled wryly. "Well, that's *not* where we live, but we do live in a cottage behind it."

"Our father is King Herod's stableman, and our mother works in his kitchen. After feasts, they let her bring food home," the older brother said.

Herod may have been notorious, but his banquets were legendary. I imagined a huge table filled with exotic meat, cheese, and fruit, then recited the local saying, "No guest ever walked away from Herod's invitation."

Jacob finished the saying with the part I didn't dare say out loud. "But if he isn't careful, he might not walk away at all." He snickered and added, "We know what people say, but he's not that bad."

I wasn't sure about that, but right then the thought of Herod's table scraps outweighed any concern about sleeping steps away from a murderer.

The older brother said, "By the way, I'm David. You can ride with me because you almost lost your life once today."

Almost losing my life was becoming an everyday occurrence, but I didn't say that. I introduced myself, threw on my sandals, and grabbed my bag.

Jacob reached for it. "I'll take that for you."

I clutched the bag, wishing David could take it, but his horse didn't have a saddlebag. I didn't understand people like Jacob who were overconfident, and I certainly didn't trust them. Too much confidence makes you careless. Meanwhile, my hesitation was probably making Jacob wonder what was in my bag.

Slowly I handed it to him. "Be very careful. These are the bones of my grandfather."

"If you say so." He grabbed my bag, then put it in his saddlebag. He probably had that horse sense which could recognize fear.

I had to let him know I wasn't intimidated. "Oh, I probably should've mentioned that I was just in contact with a leper."

Jacob ran to the shore and washed his hands.

David laughed. "I think you've met your match, Jacob."

While David held the reins, I tried to mount the horse. I put one foot in the stirrup and grabbed the horn of the saddle, but my foot slipped, and I hung on the side of the horse for a moment, kicking the air and the horse. What a first impression I made!

David helped my foot find the stirrup, and I pulled myself up, then he mounted in front of me and gave the horse the command to trot. I looked back at Jacob. Instead of following us, he and his horse cut across the river. I watched to see when he would turn toward us, but he didn't. What was he doing? The distance between my bag and me grew by the second. Had I just been swindled?

CHAPTER 16

WILD AND WILY

I thought I was going to be like one of those goats that faints and rolls onto its back with its stiff legs straight up in the air. And it was a long way down from the top of David's horse.

With my mirror bouncing in its saddlebag, Jacob's horse dashed through the field, leaving David and me behind. My heart slammed against my chest. I yelled in David's ear, "Where's Jacob going?"

David shrugged and called out, "What are you doing?"

"Winning!" Jacob yelled. Jacob's horse slowed down just long enough to show us the grin on Jacob's face, then galloped away. Jacob was wily, but he wasn't a thief.

David's horse galloped until we caught up with Jacob. The two horses rode side by side, though sometimes David's horse was forced to ride through a ditch. David and I dodged low-hanging branches from sycamore trees. The horses were neck and neck, but when the stone palace came into view, David's horse slowed down as if it didn't want to disturb the royal family. Jacob raised his arms in victory, and David raised his finger to his lips to warn him to gloat silently.

When we stopped around the back at a large stable, we all dismounted. Jacob unbuckled his saddlebag but wouldn't touch my bag after my leper comment. I lifted my bag out, listening for the tinkling of broken glass. Instead, all I heard was David's horse chomping on an apple. Believe me when I tell you that without the promise of Herod's leftovers, I would've taken it right out of its mouth.

Jacob led me inside their cottage to a back room and gave me dry clothes.

As soon as he left, I opened my bag. The mirror was intact, and the gem was still in the scroll. I just had to make it through the night, then trade the gem for a donkey in the morning.

When I came out, Jacob told me to hang my wet tunic by the fire, but I kept my bag with me. He handed me a plate with huge portions of food, and I thanked him, then silently said a blessing.

When I looked up, he was waiting to say something. "So, where are you from?"

I replied with a mouthful of goat cheese and orange jam. "A village in Galilee."

"What brings you here?" Jacob asked.

"Business in Jerusalem." I didn't dare mention Jesus since Herod had John the Baptist beheaded.

"What kind of business?"

I swigged some rose tea. "Just a delivery."

Jacob squinted. "You've come all this way by yourself?"

"I've been here many times."

"You know there are bandits on the way to Jerusalem," he said.

I bit my lip, so I wouldn't smile. Jacob worked for Herod, yet he worried about bandits?

"We prepare ourselves for encounters with bandits," he said. "Are you up for a challenge?"

I loosened the belt on my borrowed tunic. I didn't know my belly could expand that much. "Only if it's a challenge to see who can eat the most."

"Not quite," he said. "Did your mother ever tell you not to run with a dagger?"

I put a fig cake into my mouth and nodded.

"How about running with a dagger on a narrow platform thirty feet off the ground?"

I choked on some crumbs. When I coughed fitfully, Jacob hit me on the back, which he seemed to enjoy.

CHAPTER 17

MORE FUN THAN PRISON

Jacob was wrong. The platform was only twenty feet off the ground, not thirty; nonetheless, my heart didn't beat any more slowly. I had followed him to the stable and stood under the platform which connected the lofts on each end.

David was raking hay into a pile that was taller than he was. His voice echoed across the stable. "Jacob, what are you doing now?"

"Being a good host. We can't send him out on the roads unprepared." Near the back wall, a bale of straw was standing on its side, and Jacob walked over and poked it. "Pretend this is the bandit." A small red target had been drawn near the top of the bale, and a dagger protruded from it.

"I know what I'm doing," I said. "A few days ago, I used my dagger when bandits threatened to sell me into slavery." They didn't need to know any more than that.

Jacob raised an eyebrow, then went up the ladder. "What else are we going to do for fun? They won't let me in the prison anymore."

He sauntered halfway across the platform and sat down. Some careless person had neglected to install railings, so Jacob dangled his legs over the edge. "Eli, here's what you do. Climb up the ladder, run here and throw the dagger at the bale, then run to the other loft."

I tilted my head back to study the platform, then David came over and whispered, "I saw your cut feet. You don't have to do this. Who cares what Jacob thinks?"

My lips tightened into a forced smile. "I know." I strode over to the ladder and tugged on it. It seemed to be anchored securely. I pointed to the loft on the far side. "How do I get down from there? There's no ladder."

David grabbed a rope hanging from the ceiling. "I'll swing this to you. Jump on and fly across to the pile of hay."

There was no way I was taking the mirror up there, so I set my bag down on a stool. "It'll be hard to climb the ladder while holding a dagger."

"You can use my sheath," Jacob said. "In fact, if you can do this, you can keep it."

"Or you could just give me the sheath. Bandits would see it and decide to wait for a more vulnerable victim, then all this preparation would be unnecessary," I said.

"Ah, I see you like using wits instead of violence, but that's boring." He removed the leather sheath from his rope belt and threw it down.

I tried to catch it, but it smacked me in the eye. As the smell of leather entered my nostrils, Uncle Shem's favorite phrase invaded my mind and plundered my courage. "That boy falls more than sparks from a hammer."

I shook my head, then my arms and legs, hoping to limber up and cast off his insulting words. "Give me three tries."

"Fine," Jacob grumbled, descending the ladder.

I untied my rope belt, looped it through the opening of the sheath, then pulled the rope tight. I yanked the dagger out of the bale and placed it in the sheath.

In front of me, a row of horses peeked out of their stalls, eagerly watching their charioteer put me to the test. Two of them neighed, probably placing bets on my chances.

David clapped. "You can do it, Eli."

I sprinted to the ladder. As I grasped each rung, splinters pricked my palms. I looked over my shoulder at the spinning floor far below, and my body leaned back slightly. I straightened myself, turned back around, and hugged the ladder. I took a breath and climbed to the loft. Perhaps Jacob was right about it being thirty feet off the ground.

I started running. You know how they say your guardian angel is always by your side? Not this time. The platform was too narrow for anyone else.

When I looked down, the movement of my feet made it appear that the wood was heaving beneath me, so I just stared ahead to the loft on the other side and warned my knees not to bump into one another.

When I was almost to the halfway point, one foot landed on a rock and skidded along on it toward the edge. I arched my back to counter the momentum of my falling body. The rock fell to the ground. My body stopped just in time. I regained my balance and stood there.

Jacob yelled, "Throw it! Now!"

My shaky fingers removed the dagger from the sheath. I looked at the rest of the platform, which seemed to have gotten longer, then glanced at the bale of straw. I threw the dagger and took off running before I saw where it landed. Clearly it didn't hit the target because I heard the clanging of metal. In a stall below, a horse whinnied and reared up on its hind legs.

He wasn't the only one who was spooked.

As I reached the other loft, David said, "Be patient. Just do one thing at a time." He swung the rope toward me, and time seemed to slow down.

I watched the rope come closer and closer, daring me to trust it, teasing me, but it didn't come close enough to reach. I leaned out a little. There was no way to stay safely on the platform and reach it. Too bad the butterflies in my stomach couldn't help me fly. I teetered on the edge, watching the rope hurry back to David.

"Eli, relax," he said, rolling a small cart of hay under the loft to serve as a safety net. He was the last of us to lose confidence in me.

I stepped back and sighed. "Can you just throw the rope again, so I can get the timing down?"

He swung it and I silently counted the seconds it took to reach me. On the count of six, it came close, then started to recede.

I looked over at Jacob, and he did what we refer to as the *David versus Goliath* move. It's what every boy in Israel did to show dominance over an opponent in a game. He looked up at me, loaded an imaginary stone into his imaginary slingshot, pulled back, then released. He even added the sound of the stone whizzing through the air and smacking my forehead. "Now start over."

I ignored him, retraced my steps, and went down to the starting point.

David faced the target. "Try this." He put his left leg forward and held the dagger with his right hand. "Hold it in the middle, not by the hilt, and don't grip it too tight." He bent his right elbow and cocked his arm, holding the dagger behind his head and a little above. Then he extended his left arm a little lower than a Roman salute and pointed at the target. "You have the strength. Just aim with your left hand, twist your torso slightly, then release." He dropped his left arm and pretended to throw with his right.

I practiced his stance, then went through the motions of throwing several times.

Jacob yawned. "I was starting to regret my offer to reward you with my sheath, but it seems I shouldn't have worried—"

Before he could finish, I darted up the ladder and halfway across the platform. I took out the dagger, followed David's instructions, and cocked my arm. The metal hitching post that I had apparently hit the last time was a foot from the bale. I aimed my left arm at the target and threw with my right. The dagger flew through the air and stuck on the inside edge of the circle. It's amazing what happens when people give clear directions.

I ran to the platform and waited for the rope. On the count of four, I jumped toward it. Actually, I pounced on it but without the grace of a cat. My face found the rope first, and the rough fibers clawed across my cheek. My hands flailed, desperately trying to grab the rope. My pinky and a thumb caught it but couldn't hold my weight. My body hit the cart, first my back then my head.

One moment, I had been enveloped by air, the next, every bit of it was knocked out of me. I lay there motionless. The scratches on my cheek burned. Moldy-smelling hay poked my ears, arms, and legs.

The brothers peered into the cart. David's eyes were wide. "Are you hurt?"

The swagger was gone from Jacob's voice. "Maybe I should just give you the sheath."

I didn't want their pity.

David said, "In moments like this, my father always reminds me of King David's death-bed advice to his son—"

Jacob interrupted, "Oh, I know this one. He said, 'Send my enemy's head to the grave.' "

David scowled. "Not that; right before that. He said, 'Take courage and be a man.' "

I sat upright. "My father carved that on a slingshot."

He punched my shoulder. "Well, there you go. Obey your father."

Once again, perhaps more detailed instructions would have been helpful, but I got down and plodded to the back of the cart, shedding hay as I went. I pushed the cart away, so it was no longer a safety net. "Third try."

I ran up the ladder and halfway across the platform, pulled out the dagger, aimed, and threw. It impaled the bale toward the bottom of the circle, not a bullseye, but enough to stop a bandit.

I sped to the other loft and waited for the rope, wiping my sweaty hands on my tunic. The rope got closer and I leaned toward it, balancing on my toes. When I counted to six, I jumped off the platform. My fingers fumbled a moment, then grasped the rope. I held on with my thighs for extra stability.

Before the rope receded, I was suspended in midair. I mouthed the words, "Great beard of my father!" Then I soared over the brothers, and David grinned while Jacob raised his arms victoriously. I threw back my head and shouted, "Whoo!"

As I flew toward the hay pile, my stomach giggled then plunged to my feet, but I wasn't ready to get off. I swooped toward the other side of the stable. My tunic billowed, and I flew so high that my hair reached out and touched the loft.

The rope glided back down, and the horses admired my agility. On the other end of the stable, I swung close enough to touch a nest of barn swallows hidden in the joint of two beams. I went back and forth several times until the rafter holding the rope creaked as I slowed down. "David, could you give me a push?"

He launched me and when I reached the hay pile, I didn't drop onto it. I crashed through it. I emerged from the other side with pieces of straw sticking out from my smile. I was ready for bandits.

CHAPTER 18

TYRANT'S TREASURE

fter swinging on the rope, one of my all-time favorite things, I was forced into one of my least favorite things: wrestling . . . with my conscience.

As we were leaving the stable, David stopped outside the tack room. While he unlocked the door, I ran my finger along a jagged crack running down the wall.

"That's from the earthquake," Jacob said.

"I didn't know you felt it all the way down here," I said. The earthquake must have affected the entire country. Perhaps that's what Abel had been trying to tell me the day I left home.

Jacob pointed toward the horses. "Chestnut and Powder knew something was about to happen. When they refused to leave the stable, we worried my father would be beaten for not carrying out Herod's orders."

"Was he?" I asked.

"Not that time. After the earthquake, everything else was forgotten. In fact"—Jacob cupped his hand beside his mouth and lowered his voice—"the queen was so upset, she hasn't left the palace since."

David waved us into the tack room. "Shh! *You're* going to get a beating."

The tack room resembled a queen's dressing room. Colorful saddle blankets hung on the walls, some made of silk, others of velvet, some with embroidered crests and shiny, copper buckles, and some with sparkling gems.

Gems! The emerald I had found must belong to Herod! It probably fell off during one of Jacob's wild maneuvers.

If I gave the gem back, I couldn't barter for a donkey. I would have to walk all night to Jerusalem, but I was so tired, too tired to face real bandits.

To me, the emerald meant so much, but would Herod even miss it? It's not like I stole it. I found it in the crevice and worked hard to get it out. Did I have to return it? Or was it mine now?

David grabbed a jar of honey and a small brush, then turned to go. We followed him out, and he started to slide the lock across the door jamb.

I had a split second to make up my mind. I needed to return the gem right then.

The sound of the slamming metal bolt echoed throughout the stable in finality, ending my indecision. I put the strap over my shoulders and pressed the bag to my side. I was keeping the gem.

We went to the rooftop terrace where someone had put out three sleeping mats. I put my bag and sheath under a small table in case it rained, then sat on the mat Jacob designated as mine.

David handed me a jar of honey and the brush. "We use this for all kinds of wounds. Try it on your feet."

I thanked him and opened the jar, releasing the scent of roses. Jacob watched me dunk the brush into the honey and self-consciously lift it from the jar to my feet, dripping honey along the way. The horsehair bristles tickled my skin, but the honey soothed the cuts.

David handed me linen strips to wrap my feet. "Just leave these on all night."

I wrapped my feet and lay on the mat.

Jacob started walking backwards toward my bag. "Since you're not going anywhere with those mummified feet, let's see what's really in your bag."

He would find the gem! They'd accuse me of stealing it. I'd end up in their prison. "No!" I yelled, scrambling to my feet.

"Jacob!" David scolded.

Jacob strutted back to his mat. "I'm joking. After seeing you throw that dagger, I'm not messing with you."

I lay back down and watched the white clouds cover up the moon. When I traded the gem for a donkey, would the merchant accuse me of stealing it from Herod? How else would a boy like me have a beautiful emerald?

My mat was soft, and my stomach was full. They had been good hosts, but I wished I had never met them, so I wouldn't have second thoughts about keeping the gem.

The lids were closed over Jacob's *I-dare-you* eyes, and his smirk collapsed into parted lips that exhaled rhythmically like a baby. Would Herod's men beat them when they realized the gem was missing?

I thought about Jacob, not Jacob of Jericho, but Jacob, the Father of the Twelve Tribes of Israel, as I wrestled my conscience until daybreak.

CHAPTER 19

ACCUSING EYES

How can you tell if someone's shifty? Is it his overly excited voice or his darting eyes? These are just a couple of the thoughts I grappled with as the sun rose the next morning. After finally overcoming all my objections about keeping the gem, I just needed to find a shifty merchant who wouldn't question whether the gem had been stolen from Herod.

I glanced at Jacob for clues about tricky people, but his sleeping face was no help.

Right then, David brought me a pail of warm water and a clean towel.

I thanked him and unraveled the linen strips on my feet, revealing that the cuts were no longer bright red or swollen. I washed off the honey and slowly stood up. "Great beard of my father, that feels better."

David handed me my clothes. "One of the fringes fell off as my mother was washing the cloak."

Jacob sat up. "Who wears fringes anymore, anyway?"

I noticed for the first time that he didn't have fringes hanging on the corners of his cloak. "I thought all true Israelites did," I said.

David gave me the braided blue and white strand, identical to each of the four fringes on his cloak. "They're supposed to make us remember God's commands."

"Well, Pharisees wear them, and it means nothing," Jacob said.

I didn't have time to defend the Pharisees. After David and Jacob left the terrace, I changed into my tunic, then attached the fringe to my cloak and the sheath to my belt.

Downstairs Jacob offered me a bowl of rice and raisins, but I shook my head. "I need to get to Jerusalem by the sixth hour."

His gaping mouth was about to tell me that was impossible on foot, but someone banged on the door, then barged in. "Jacob, Herod needs Chestnut at the main palace right away. David, his daughter wants Powder ready for her morning ride. Now!"

David jumped up and I followed him to the stable, hoping to quickly say goodbye.

Jacob ran up behind me. "Your fringe fell off again." He threw it to me, then sprinted back outside.

I didn't have time to reattach it.

David was in the first stall, putting a pink saddle blanket on a horse. Somewhere there was a saddle blanket with a discolored patch of fabric where an emerald used to be. When would Herod's men discover that the gem was missing?

I opened my bag to put the fringe in, and the dead locust looked up at me with accusing eyes. If Jacob had criticized the holy leaders of Israel for being hypocrites, what would they say about me, a professed "true Israelite," if they ever found out I had kept the gem? I couldn't do it.

I slowly removed the emerald from the scroll. The light shining through the windows made it gleam. I rubbed the smooth surface for the last time. "I found this gem in the river. It must belong to Herod."

David was adjusting a strap under the horse's belly and didn't even look up. "Oh, you can just put it down on that pail," referring to a rusty overturned bucket in the corner from which it could be easily knocked off, falling into the deep, dirty hay, lost forever.

I stared at him. What a different world these people lived in.

After David walked the horse out of the stable, I placed the gem on the old bucket, then slowly took off the sheath Jacob had given me and left it next to the gem. I put Timon's dagger in my bag. If I was robbed by bandits, so be it. At least that would be a good excuse for not delivering the mirror on time. Yesterday's victory meant nothing. I should've returned the gem right away, then walked all night to Jerusalem. I fell to my knees. *Dear God, please help me!*

I got up slowly, went outside, thanked David for his hospitality, and started shuffling toward Jerusalem. The entire weight of my body settled at my ankles. I was tired of propping up my optimism.

CHAPTER 20

SEARCHING WITHIN THE WALLS

ither Jacob was tricking me, or God answered my prayer quickly. Suddenly, he rode up. I mean Jacob, not God.

"Eli, you can ride with me," he said, panting. "To Jerusalem. Hurry, because I must be there in an hour."

"You're going to Jerusalem?" I asked.

"That's where the main palace is. I wasn't joking about bandits on the way, and you're as nimble as a billy goat."

"I'll be right back." I ran inside the stable, grabbed the sheath, looped my rope belt through it, and put Timon's dagger inside. The gem was still sitting on the bucket, and I thanked God that I didn't need it.

I mounted Jacob's horse without falling, and off we rode. Speaking of being more nimble than a billy goat, that horse expertly jumped logs and creeks as he galloped. *Isn't it just like God to provide a racehorse when you prayed for a donkey?*

The wind carried the smell of balsam fir trees as it whipped against my face. Soon the green grass and palm trees of Jericho gave way to desolate, rocky ground. The route was uphill nearly the entire way, and the horse often slowed to climb some steep terrain. If any bandits spotted us, surely, they were deterred by my sheath.

We almost crested the Mount of Olives when I saw the golden tips of the Temple in the distance.

Jacob reined in the horse. "Chestnut needs a rest before we go down to the valley."

I jumped off and ran to the top of the hill, taking in a sweeping view of Jerusalem on the other side of the Kidron Valley. You didn't have to be a treasure hunter to spot the Temple. The sun made its white marble walls glisten. Its massive columns were topped with a flourish of shiny gold so that they resembled torches. Above the columns was a ribbon of ornately carved gold, and golden tips crowned the roof.

The Temple was much taller than it was wide, as though it stretched to reach heaven. Giving it a boost was the gigantic rectangular base built on Mount Moriah. When we brought the Ark back, the Temple would no longer have to stretch to reach God. It would stand even taller because God was inside.

Jacob interrupted my thoughts. "You've seen it before, right?"

I didn't take my eyes off the Temple. "You know, other countries build amazing structures, but only Israel uses its engineering and artistic brilliance for the home of the one true God."

"All because of Herod the Great," he said.

That wasn't entirely true, but arguing would take away from my moment. Jerusalem looked as exciting as ever. What had Abel been trying to tell me about it?

I remounted and the horse trudged down to the valley. Jacob directed it around to the west side of the city.

I covered my nose with my cloak. "What's that smell?"

"We're approaching the Valley of Hinnom," Jacob said.

A man stood on the steep cliff above the valley, emptying a bucket of garbage. How was it possible for a city less than one square mile to produce a whole valley full of trash? On my mental list of the worst possible jobs, I added the job *garbage tender at Hinnom* right below the words *Uncle Shem's apprentice*.

The horse climbed up the slope, and I bent my neck back to see the top of the massive stone wall which surrounded Jerusalem and defended its exclusivity. Of course, Romans had bullied their way in, and though their fortress and spy towers stood their ground, they would never belong.

Herod's gate was so tall, I could've stood on top of the horse and still wouldn't have needed to duck. After passing through, we dismounted and Herod's local stableman led the horse away.

I set my bag down, took out the scroll, and read directions to the customer's house:

HOUSE OF EZRA BAR SIMON
UPPER CITY, JERUSALEM

Those were vague directions. Was Uncle Shem purposely making this difficult? Just find the exact house of one man amongst the ninety thousand people that lived in Jerusalem. Of course, finding Jesus, who didn't even have a house, would be much harder.

Jacob leaned in, attempting to read the scroll. "Let's go see a chariot race before I head back."

"No, I have to make the delivery."

Despite his desire to take in the local entertainment, Jacob followed me as I strode toward the Upper City, looking for someone who could tell me where to find Ezra or Jesus. An annoyed merchant chased a wan beggar away from his wine stand. In front of a fish stand, two little girls teased their cat with some fish bones. If Jesus was in the city, these people either didn't know or didn't care.

From the square, I went down a narrow, winding street which turned into a stony pathway. The pathway meandered beneath many arches until it ended at a huge tower that practically blocked out the sun— the sun which kept moving, reminding me that I was running out of time. I stopped abruptly, shaking my head, and Jacob bumped into me.

"*Consiste!*" a voice barked in Latin from the top of the tower.

I didn't have to speak Latin to know that meant stop. "Sorry, I'm lost," I said, hoping the Roman soldier spoke Aramaic as well.

"Stay right there," he commanded in Aramaic. He walked back into the tower and out of sight, then emerged from the street-level doorway and stood right in front of us. "I saw you two ride in. Did you pay the publican yet?"

Was this conversation like the meandering pathway: innocent-looking but leading to a dead end?

CHAPTER 21

WHAT TO BELIEVE

My view at that moment was a shiny, metal breastplate. Why did they engrave fake muscles on the breastplates when Romans had plenty of real ones? But the soldier was the one asking the questions, and I didn't have answers. And I didn't have money to pay the publican.

Jacob took out a small, round piece of wax with Herod's seal on it. "We're exempt from the tax because I'm on official business for Herod."

The soldier pivoted out of the way. "In that case, please proceed."

My papa always said that people of all races really want to help when they see someone in need. I wasn't sure about that, but I was desperate. "Can you tell me how to get to the house of Ezra bar Simon in the Upper City? I'm on a critical mission."

"I have a friend staying at Ezra's inn," he said. "Normally you could get there quickly, but they just brought sheep into the market, and it's mayhem over there. Would you like me to show you a shortcut?"

I replied with more confidence than I felt. "I'd be very grateful."

The soldier fastened the strap of his bronze helmet, then another soldier yelled down at him from the tower, "Longinus!"

Longinus frowned and replied to the soldier in Latin.

Jacob grinned and translated for me. "He said he wouldn't get caught this time."

Longinus put his finger to his lips. "Follow me." Before I could reply, he rushed into the Hippicus Tower, his cape fanning out behind him. Apparently, Romans didn't wait for subordinates to object.

Jacob followed him into the tower.

What was in there? A jail? A torture chamber? I looked around to see if anyone would hear us if we shouted for help.

A Pharisee and a guard were walking past. Surely, the Pharisee would know where to find Jesus. After so many near misses, I needed a credible lead.

Jacob came back to the doorway. "What are you waiting for?"

I pointed to the Pharisee. "I need to ask him something."

"That's Malachi. He likes to think that he's the Holy of Holies. Let's go." Jacob tried to wave me into the tower. "What about your critical mission?"

He had a point, but I couldn't pass up an opportunity to talk to an expert who could help me find Jesus. Besides, I still had a little time left to deliver the mirror.

The Pharisee stopped in the middle of the road and bent over to pray, so I ran to catch up with him. He remained in silent prayer for several minutes while the guard looked straight ahead. I waited and waited, tapping my fingers on my bag and wondering if Rabbi Malachi planned to say all 150 psalms.

Finally, he stood upright, then opened his eyes. He jumped, seeing me directly in front of him, then extended his arm and swept it out in front of his body to show that I was standing too close.

I couldn't blame him. Though my tunic was clean, my hair was messy, and who knows how dirty my face was. After all, I didn't dare use the mirror I was delivering. I took two steps back.

He began walking, so I caught up and matched his stride. "Peace be upon you, Rabbi Malachi. May I ask you a question, please?"

Barely moving his head, he glanced at me out of the corner of his eye. "I'm in a very big hurry."

"I promise not to slow you down," I said. "Can you just tell me where I can find Jesus?"

Rabbi Malachi stooped down and stuck out his neck, so his face was just inches from mine, close enough for me to see the color of his eyes, brownish-red like dried blood. "What did you say?" he asked.

"Is Jesus here in Jerusalem?"

Rabbi Malachi stood back up. He straightened his phylactery, the small leather box strapped to his forehead that contained verses about how God brought our people out of bondage in Egypt. "Why yes, we'll take you to Him."

I rubbed my hands together. With his help, my odds of meeting Jesus were far better than 1 in 90,000. Jacob was leaning against the doorway of the tower, and I yelled back at him. "They're going to show me something. Thanks for the ride."

He sprinted to me. "I'll go along in case you encounter bandits." He opened his eyes wide. "If you know what I mean."

I shook my head and sighed. It would do Jacob good to meet Jesus. I quickly wiped my face with my cloak and smoothed down my hair.

We walked out a gate located south of the one we had just come in. I had figured Jesus would be at the Temple, but perhaps we were getting a private meeting. I had so much to talk to Him about. I felt like a stone loaded in a slingshot. Every part of me was expectant, not just the treasure hunter or the reluctant apprentice, but the devout Israelite and the impatient pilgrim.

We stopped outside the city walls, and Rabbi Malachi pointed to the guard. "As is the custom, give him your sheath, dagger, and bag."

I handed them over to the guard who placed the dagger and sheath inside my bag, then put the strap of my bag over his head and onto his shoulder.

Rabbi Malachi smiled. "Now Jesus will know that you're not violent or attached to material things."

"Jesus?" Jacob asked. "What are you talking about?"

I whispered, "Jacob, don't show disrespect." I looked around, expecting Jesus to walk up.

Jacob's green eyes filled with compassion. "I can't believe you didn't know."

I made myself say, "Know what?" but somehow I seemed too far away to hear myself. My heart began to beat too loudly, and the words my new friend spoke next made no sense.

"Jesus was crucified. Two months ago."

I staggered backwards as if Jacob had punched me in the gut. *Crucified? What kind of horrible joke was he trying to play on me?*

"No, no, no! That can't be," I said. *How could Jesus be dead?* My thoughts whirled out of control as a sinking feeling swallowed my soul.

Crucified?

Crucified. Jesus?

Crucified!

The horrible words stabbed me like daggers.

I tried to put up a shield of reason. *How could men kill God?* A blurry Malachi was smirking at me through the hot tears in my eyes. Then he moved in for the kill.

"Jesus *was* crucified, and Israel is better off." He grabbed my wrist, digging his fingernails into my skin while the guard grabbed Jacob.

I unlocked Malachi's fishhook fingers and twisted his arm until his face contorted with pain and he squealed, "Help me!"

The guard let go of Jacob and pushed me to the ground. I lay on my back, watching Jacob run away until Malachi kicked dirt in my face. Dust sprayed my eyes, and I tasted gravel.

The guard crouched down, pressing his knees into my ribs. "Should I go after him?" he asked Malachi.

"Let him go. He's not one of them," Malachi said.

I wriggled in the dirt to get out from underneath the guard, but he yanked my arms and slammed my wrists together—more grinding of bone on bone— then Malachi tied my wrists in front of me and pulled the rope tight, making the fibers burn into my skin. The guard put shackles on my feet, then lifted me up by my wrists, causing scorching pain in my shoulders.

I looked at Malachi and shouted, "You hypocrite! Did you kill Jesus?"

He shrugged his shoulders. "Humility is a virtue. I can't take all the credit."

Despite my shackled feet, I managed to hop toward him, jabbing my bound fists into his proud chin, then hearing his teeth bang together. We fell to the ground and flailed like fish.

The whack of a club triggered an intense sting radiating from the back of my knees up to my neck. I closed my eyes and the guard pulled me up by my hair.

With the help of the guard, Malachi stood up and wiped the sweat from his forehead using the striped border of his cloak. He rolled up his wide sleeves, revealing grayish skin like that of a dwarf snake.

I tottered for a moment, then fixed my eyes on his. "God will avenge His Son sevenfold."

The guard sneered. "We're expecting hail and fire to rain down any second." He stuffed a rag in my mouth.

Malachi chuckled and went behind me. "Walk, heathen." Then he shoved me so hard I doubled over.

I regained my balance, and the guard led me away from the city to the cliff overlooking the Valley of Hinnom.

Malachi started to speak, making a whistling sound each time he said a word with the letter *s*. "Israel must not repeat her mistakes. Why doesn't your father teach you those things?"

I flinched.

He continued, "This is the Valley of Slaughter, so called because rebellious Israelites worshiped false gods and threw their children into fires here as a sacrificial offering. Since you insist upon worshiping a false god, go to your sacrifice."

Then he pushed me off the cliff.

CHAPTER 22

THE VALLEY OF SLAUGHTER

or years I had told myself just to hang on a little longer until the Messiah made every-thing better. Malachi had just severed the worn thread by which I'd been hanging.

Hands and feet grasping at the air.

Internal organs rising as if to escape.

Soul pleading with God, then bracing for—

IMPACT!

The force of my body smacking the landfill made the garbage ripple out. When my flight finally came to a stop, the refuse filled back in between my toes, in my armpits, and under my chin.

Above me, Malachi flicked the dirt off his fingers. "One more poisonous mushroom ripped out." The guard handed him my bag, and they headed back toward the city.

I craned my neck, watching my bag get farther and farther away until they were out of sight and probably back within the city walls.

Those massive walls hadn't protected Jerusalem from the worst assault in history. The evil was already inside, an evil strong enough to kill God.

I imagined Jesus being led out of those walls to the desolate site where all the crucifixions took place. I pictured Him.

Hanging on a cross.

Blood pouring down His arms from the nail holes.

Malachi and others taunting Him.

Perhaps Jesus saw the Temple in the distance and decided that if all its leaders were like Malachi, the Ark of the Covenant was better off in a solitary cave. Israel had lost the Divine Presence for good.

No! a firm voice screamed inside my aching head. *Jesus* must *have known that very few Israelites were like Malachi.*

I hoped, I prayed, that Jesus witnessed the people who tried to defend Him.

Even so, life already seemed back to normal in Jerusalem. *Why weren't they still mourning? And why didn't they stone Malachi and the other murderers?*

Better yet, my own voice seemed to scream back at the other voice, *why didn't God pour down His wrath?* Mama always emphasized God's mercy, but I preferred His justice.

Then again, maybe it was God's mercy that kept Mama and me from being in Jerusalem that day. After Papa died, she put her heart back together hastily, using whatever she could salvage, and it couldn't have endured what her eyes would've seen. Who had told her about Jesus's death? Hopefully, Abel and not Uncle Shem—

This is what Abel had been trying to tell me that day I left home!

The news of Jesus's crucifixion must've spread quickly, but I had been watching over Mama and hadn't seen anybody for weeks. No wonder Abel was so insistent!

But I was too impatient.

I banged my two fists as one, back and forth, side to side on the garbage, and gooey, brown liquid splattered my cheeks and wrists, seeping into my wounds:

scratches carved by the rope in Jacob's stable, and new cuts rendered by the current bindings. When I lifted my hands to my face, I thought I was hallucinating. The fibers of the rope were moving! When I realized it was covered with squirming maggots, my throat tightened and I began to salivate, signaling that my stomach was about to be emptied. With the rag still firmly in my mouth and my hands bound, I would surely choke to death if that happened.

Breathing slowly and evenly through my nose, I willed the feeling to go away, then shook my stiff arms as best I could until most of the maggots fell off. The smell of animal waste and rotten fruit was enough to make me want to stop breathing, but—

Mama!

She was probably counting down the days until I returned.

And poor Tamar was still holding out hope for Jesus. And Abel was giving up on finding the Ark. Somewhere out there, Uncle Shem's customer was wondering when his mirror would arrive. I should've delivered it right away.

A buzzard flew high above me, and with only my head sticking out of the garbage, I must've looked like a hedgehog. I leaned my head back and a rotten water-melon caved in around it. I was more of a captive than ever, but without the hope that Jesus could set me free.

I closed my eyes. When I inhaled, my throat moaned and vibrated with the effort of holding back tears. I would never meet Jesus. The time of the Messiah was over, and I missed it. And like Jesus, I was going to die before I accomplished my mission.

I lay there for several minutes. The skin on my wrists was burning from the rope. Last time I got a rope burn, David had told me to take courage and be a man. Papa had told me the same thing years ago when I wasn't even close to being a man.

Papa!

I opened my eyes. I couldn't give up. Papa would want me to find a way out. No matter what!

Though I was suspended in the garbage, if I could push off the bottom of the valley, maybe I could pro-pel myself closer to the steep walls and somehow climb up. I kicked my feet to break the shackles, but they didn't budge.

Suddenly, smoke rose from the other end of the valley. A garbage tender stood on the cliff, throwing a torch into the ravine. I tried yelling for help, but the rag in my mouth prevented the sounds from becoming decipherable words. He kept walking and throwing torches.

The wind swept away streams of smoke from the places where the torches were igniting the garbage. Soon flames rose from three different piles of burning rubbish. The flames from each pile scrambled to meet the other piles like a mob of angry, torch-wielding rioters banding together. Then they started coming toward me, accelerating through the layers and layers of perfect kindling.

I pointed my toes and stretched my legs to try to reach the bottom of the valley. It was too deep. I tried to bend my torso forward, then jerk it back and bounce toward the valley walls. Despite exerting all my strength, I was barely moving. The flames crept to within six feet. My face grew hotter, but my body had goosebumps. Beads of sweat dripped from my forehead and tickled my nose.

I prayed for a fiery chariot to whisk me away like it carried the prophet Elijah.

Instead, God sent a fiery *charioteer.*

A voice shouted, "There he is!" I twisted my neck to see Longinus and Jacob standing behind me on the cliff.

Longinus perfectly aimed and threw one end of a rope so that it landed where my two wrists were fixed together as one. I somehow managed to grab hold. As they lifted me, the garbage made a slurping sound. Clumps of curdled milk and onion peels fell off while I dangled in the air. As I inched up, so did the flames. My legs were getting hot, but I was high enough to see their faces straining as they pulled the rope. Finally, my elbows balanced on the edge, and Jacob dragged me up by my armpits, then took the rag out of my mouth.

My dry tongue fumbled to form words. "You got here just in time." Down in the valley, the fire devoured the watermelon I had used for a headrest.

As I sat on the ground shaking, Longinus cut the ropes off my wrists.

He examined the shackles on my feet, then dug in his bag, retrieved a long pin and placed it in the lock. He turned the pin and nothing happened. He squinted, then alternated jiggling and turning the pin. Finally, the shackles fell off. "You showed all the fortitude of a Roman, boy."

"And you showed all the kindness of an Israelite," I replied.

His lips tightened in a wry smile.

"Well, certain Israelites. I mean . . . uh . . ." I was better off with a rag in my mouth. "What I really wanted to say is thank you. Thank you both. How did you find me?"

Jacob backed away from me and covered his nose with his cloak. "Longinus was watching from the tower when I ran back to ask for help."

I peered up at Longinus—way up so I could look him in the eyes. "I'm sorry I didn't follow you into the tower. Apparently, I'm not a good judge of character."

Longinus unfastened his cape. "I'm used to being wrongly judged by people on this side of the world." He took the lid off his waterskin and poured water on the cape, then handed it to me. "These days even other Romans don't understand me."

I thanked him, then wiped my face, hair, clothes, and feet. "I have to get my bag from Malachi some-how. Do you know where he lives?"

"You can bet he wouldn't step inside his palace after being in contact with people like us," Longinus said.

"You're right. He must be purifying himself at the mikveh right now." I handed the filthy cape back to him. "Do you know a shortcut?"

Longinus put his cape into his bag. "Not this time, so let's hurry."

We rushed back into the city and down the narrow street that I had walked up a short time ago. Back when I was expectant. And ignorant.

CHAPTER 23

WITS OR VIOLENCE

Three things evoked fear in every Israelite: an emerging leprous sore on a loved one, a house fire in a row of connected houses, and a Roman soldier's footprint outside the door. Unlike the smooth-surfaced soles of Israelite sandals, the soles of Roman soldiers' shoes were covered with nailheads. That day, those nailhead footprints in the dusty lane represented hope as Jacob and I followed Longinus to the mikveh where we could take my bag back from Malachi.

Longinus had a long stride. My short stride created footprints beside and in between each of his footprints. Jacob didn't bother to jog to keep up. People moved out of Longinus's way, and when someone left a cart directly in his path, he jumped over it. I turned around and looked at Jacob who smiled in amusement and raised his arm, giving me the Roman salute. Then I walked *around* the cart.

The mikveh was just south of the Temple, but I forced myself not to look at the Temple's gleaming walls in the distance because it would only remind me of Jesus. I didn't have time to mourn right then. I needed a plan to get my bag back.

We approached the circus where gladiator fights and chariot races took place. It was a long building with curved ends to accommodate the track inside. Suddenly, Roman footprints inspired my plan. "Longinus, can you get me a gladiator shoe?"

"You mean a pair?"

"No, just one."

"Certainly. You can always count on there being extra shoes lying around after gladiator fights." Longinus pushed open the door and stepped inside the circus.

Jacob glanced at me and I stopped biting my fingernails. "Why go to all this trouble?" he asked. "What's really in your bag?"

"Just something I'm delivering for my uncle, and if I don't deliver it on time, he'll be the first to affirm that I belong in that garbage pit."

"Then what's the plan? Are we using wits or violence?" Jacob asked.

"We'll try the truth, then resort to trickery if we have to. This is only going to work if Malachi went directly to the mikveh and is still there. If he purified himself quickly and went home, I'll never get my bag back."

"Well, if he stopped to pray in front of the houses of the other seventy Sanhedrin members, we'll catch up with him," Jacob said.

Longinus came out and handed me a gladiator shoe. The sole was wedge-shaped and covered with spikes to help a gladiator grip the ground. And it was authentic. Across the top of the crisscrossed strips of leather were drops of blood. Just one more thing to contaminate me. I needed the mikveh far more than Malachi did.

I handed the shoe back to Longinus and explained the plan while we walked toward the mikveh. We stopped outside the House of Counsel, where the scribes interpreted the laws. For someone wanting to appear righteous, this was the place to be seen. That made it even harder to spot Malachi because everybody wore a phylactery and a flowing headdress.

I peeked around the corner of the building. As a man stooped over to pray, his tunic went up in the back, revealing skinny grayish legs. My bag hung around his neck and dangled between his folded body and folded hands.

I whispered, "There he is."

Malachi stood upright, looking left and right to see who had noticed his pious act. He adjusted my bag so that it hung at his side, then walked into the mikveh.

We followed him but waited to go in, calculating how much time it would take Malachi to give my bag to the attendant, hang his clothes inside the changing room, walk through the door to the pool room, go down the steps into the pool, and submerge himself. For the next few minutes, I exhaled loudly, though I didn't realize it was loud until Jacob frowned at me.

Finally, I said, "Let's go."

Longinus waited outside while Jacob and I went into the changing room. The attendant was standing next to three hooks, one with my bag on it, one with

Malachi's purple cloak and robe, and one with his headdress.

"Peace be upon you." I pointed to my bag. "We're here to get this bag from Rabbi Malachi."

The attendant shook his head. "I'm not supposed to disturb him. He's been contaminated and will be in there awhile."

"That's why we're here. The bag was also in contact with a leper. He doesn't want to get contaminated again, and I have to deliver it," I said, feeling good that all of those points were true.

He wrinkled his nose at my tunic, which looked like moldy bread. "I can see you're contaminated, but why would I believe you?"

"Because I can describe the contents of the bag: a sheath, a dagger, a scroll, ostrich feathers, a dead locust—"

The attendant waved his hand in front of my face. "That's enough. I need Rabbi Malachi to verify your story."

Jacob showed his wax seal. "I'm on official business with Herod."

"And we have to deliver this bag to the Upper City right away. Open it. You'll see I'm telling the truth," I added.

"Go outside and wait at the exit door," the attendant said.

"I'll just ask him myself." I ran through the door and halfway down the pool steps.

Malachi was wading in the corner of the pool.

The attendant chased after me. "You can't come in here."

I jumped off the steps, creating the biggest splash possible. I stayed underwater and watched the distorted image of the attendant on the steps, hoping to distract him long enough to give Jacob time to grab my bag.

After the attendant came down two steps, I poked my head out of the water.

"Get out!" he yelled, lifting the hem of his tunic and coming one step closer. The water came up to his calf. While his other foot was in midair, he hesitated and looked at his tunic. "You're not worth it." He ran back up the steps and out to the changing room.

I turned around to face Malachi.

His jaw had dropped open and a small wave nearly entered his mouth. "You?" With no headdress or outer garments, he looked very small.

"Are you surprised to see me here?" I asked. "I have people looking out for me. Powerful people."

The only sound was water dripping from his beard, and his silence emboldened me. "I need to be cleansed because a few days ago I was in contact with a leper. I bet you wish you hadn't grabbed me."

"You're lying," he said.

"I'm sure there's nothing for you to worry about. Doesn't the Sanhedrin teach that leprosy is a consequence of sinfulness?" I imitated Uncle Shem's best sarcastic tone. "Surely, you haven't done anything to offend God, have you?"

Malachi's teeth started to chatter. "Of course not."

"Jesus healed so many lepers." I shook my head in mock sorrow. "What a pity He's not here to save you."

As I advanced to the middle of the pool, the sun slipped through a crack in the roof directly overhead and shone in my eyes. That meant that it was the sixth hour, the deadline for delivering the mirror! I couldn't waste any more time on Malachi.

I swiped the water, casting a wave toward him. He cowered as water poured over his head. Long strands of hair stuck to his cheeks and neck, and he wiped his eyes with his wrinkled fingers.

I swam to the exit stairs and turned around before going out the door. "When God vindicates His Son, just remember this: Israel will be better off."

Outside, Jacob was standing by the exit with my bag in his hands. Longinus had finished wedging the gladiator shoe underneath the entrance door, and we watched to see if it would stand firm. We heard the attendant's footsteps getting closer, then the door started to open, but the wedged shoe prevented it from opening more than an inch.

The attendant banged on it. "Open this door!" His fingers grasped the side of the door, but nothing else could fit through. He'd have to go back in, wade through the pool, and head out the exit, but by then we'd be gone.

Jacob handed me the bag, and I cradled it as we ran halfway across the city. In between breaths, I shouted, "Great beard of my father! It worked!" We stopped outside the amphitheater and I checked inside the bag. The mirror was still intact, and I silently thanked God.

Longinus patted me on the back. "That was a well-executed plan."

"Can you show me how to get to Ezra's now?" I asked.

Jacob's words rushed out. "Let's take the shortcut!"

Longinus put his hands up, giving the universal sign for *hold on*. "Ezra's is only a short walk from here, and the sheep aren't blocking the way anymore."

"Just tell us how you would've done it," Jacob said.

Longinus pointed to the city wall. "The shortcut is up there. We were going to run along the top of the wall."

We looked up at the wall that ran along the back of the amphitheater alongside the Upper City. It was forty feet high.

For once Jacob seemed unsure. "I didn't even know that was a possibility unless you're a soldier."

The wall seemed to sway as I stared at the top. "There's no railing."

Longinus started walking away. "It might not be permitted, but it is possible."

Jacob stood there, continuing to stare at it. "If you say so."

Perhaps there was still a bit of a treasure hunter left in me, because I tucked away that information where I could find it later.

CHAPTER 24

CUSTOMER EXPECTATIONS

I knew we were in the *right* place when I felt *out* of place. We had run through the Lower City with its small limestone houses, screaming children, and bickering merchants, but the white marble villas and mansions of the Upper City demanded dignified behavior.

Longinus and Jacob stood behind me as I knocked on Ezra's door. Was I too late? Had the customer already left town? The only sound was the bubbling fountain in the courtyard.

A few moments passed, then a man wearing a bright white tunic opened the door and spoke very slowly. "Peace be upon you all. Longinus, it's good to see you."

Longinus displayed perfect Roman efficiency. "Ezra, this is Eli. He has a delivery."

I spoke as quickly but politely as possible. "Peace be upon you. Shem bar Jude, the metalsmith from Galilee, sent me."

"Ah, yes. In that case the delivery is for Gaspar, one of my guests," Ezra said.

"Is he still here?" I asked, wiping my sweaty palms on my tunic.

"Yes, he's next door with the Div—"

Longinus cleared his throat, interrupting Ezra. "You mean he's visiting the neighbors."

Ezra's eyes widened. "Uh, yes. That's right. The neighbors."

Longinus placed his hand on my shoulder. "We'll just wait for Gaspar outside."

We stood at the corner of Ezra's house. My brief swim in the mikveh hadn't removed all the grime from Hinnom, and I scraped away an orange stain on my sleeve. "I'm a little embarrassed to meet this customer, looking the way I do."

Jacob looked me over. "It's not that bad . . . well, maybe I should let you wear my cloak."

Longinus walked to an elevated water storage tank between Ezra's inn and the neighbors. "That just might work. One time I modified a water tank so we could fill the circus for naval reenactments. Stand under here and I'll try to get the water flowing."

I handed my bag to Jacob. "Can I trust you to hold this?"

Jacob grabbed it. "After everything that's happened, you still don't trust me?"

"You're right. Sorry, I'm just anxious to finish my job."

I stood under the water tank, then Longinus pulled on a chain which opened a small door. The water poured out onto my shoulders with tremendous force, nearly pushing me to the ground. Through the torrent, I could see him tugging other chains until the water flowed gently. I scrubbed my hair and my tunic then inside my ears, under my chin, and between my toes.

A boy had started to walk past but stopped so suddenly his turban almost fell off. The sight of a person washing himself and the clothes on his back under a man-made waterfall attracted attention. "Huh. I must take that idea back to my country," he said with a strange accent.

Longinus pulled a chain to close the door of the tank and stop the water flow. "Gaspar, we've been waiting for you."

Standing there dripping, I was relieved that Uncle Shem's customer wasn't what I expected. He was just a boy, a little older than I was, with dark skin, a white turban, and a purple robe tied with a gold silk belt. It must've taken fifty thousand shells to get that robe such a deep purple.

"Ezra told us you were at the neighbor's, then nearly revealed the family secret," Longinus said.

The gold ring on Gaspar's finger glistened as he pointed to the two-story house next door. "Oh, they have not met the neighbors yet?"

"No, Eli just arrived with a delivery for you."

"Right, right, right. Welcome." With Gaspar's accent, welcome sounded like *velcome*. He motioned for us to follow him inside Ezra's inn, but Longinus explained that he had to get back to work.

I stopped walking to give Longinus my full respect. "Thank you for everything: pulling me from the garbage, letting me use your cape, wedging the gladiator shoe, and getting me here on time."

Gaspar's dark brown eyes shone with curiosity.

"You're welcome. It was an adventure," Longinus said. Jacob saluted him, and he saluted back.

Once inside, Gaspar had a servant bring me a towel. Ezra strolled down a long hallway to the foyer, then stood behind Gaspar, waiting to see what I was delivering. Jacob stood next to me, watching closely.

I set my bag down on the mosaic floor and pulled out the mirror. I removed the ostrich feathers, protective wood layers, and woolen cloth, trying not to show that my fingers were shaking. As I handed the mirror to Gaspar, I did a quick visual inspection, hoping it bore no signs of being jostled, stolen, or nearly trampled.

Gaspar held up the mirror, and I held my breath, waiting to see if he was pleased.

Jacob gave a short whistle of admiration. "That's why you were so secretive."

I quickly nodded, then tried to read Gaspar's mind, but what did I know about wealthy foreigners?

He rotated the mirror several times, scrutinizing it. He ran his fingers along the face, then took the

woolen cloth and erased his fingerprint. He turned it
over and read the inscription that Uncle Shem had
engraved on the back:

WE ARE ONLY WHAT WE ARE
IN THE EYES OF GOD
AND NOTHING MORE.

He nodded his head. "Yes, indeed." After several
moments, he said, "It is perfect for my sister."

At last I could exhale.

Gaspar handed the mirror to Ezra, then left the
room. Ezra held it in his delicate hands and looked
at his reflection. He stuck out his tongue and giggled.
He moved the mirror toward his mouth and the glass
fogged up. "Would you look at that!" Then he held it
high above his head and rubbed a bald spot that he
apparently didn't know existed. "The reflection is so
much better than on polished bronze."

I stood a little taller. "This is the first of its kind to
be made in Israel."

"Tell Shem he is a skilled craftsman. I'm pleased
he has finally made something of himself," Ezra said.

What did he mean by that? It reminded me of something Timon had said about Uncle Shem trying to convince people that he had changed.

Before I could ask Ezra to explain, Gaspar returned with silver coins and counted out thirty-one. "Thirty for Shem and an extra for you."

"Thank you." That meant I could rent a donkey for part of the way home. But did I really want to get home faster? Did I want to rush back to being Slap-dash, the apprentice?

Ezra's towel hung over my shoulders, and I didn't realize that I had been twisting the ends tightly. I relaxed my grip, then pulled off the towel to dry the puddles I had left on the mosaic floor. Tan and light blue tiles had been arranged to look like bread and fish, which reminded me of Jesus.

There was a spot in my soul where I had placed my hope of meeting Him. I blew all the air out of my mouth, releasing that last bit of hope. Suddenly, I felt unsteady and sat down on the floor, pretending to arrange the ostrich feathers and woolen wrappings in my bag.

The hopeless air hung there, making the room feel awkward until Jacob said to Gaspar, "So, where are you from?"

"Eastern Persia."

"What brought you here?" Jacob asked.

"My grandfather had traveled to this land to visit the infant Jesus, so after hearing about Him my whole life, I was so happy to finally come here and meet Him," Gaspar said.

I looked up. "I was hoping to meet Jesus, but I arrived too late."

Gaspar put his hand out to help me up. "Then you must meet Jesus's mother."

"He has a mother?"

CHAPTER 25

FAMILY SECRET

Persians might call this an epiphany, Israelites a revelation, and treasure hunters would call it a breakthrough. It was as though this foreigner handed me a map to an unexplored world when he told me that I could meet Jesus's mother.

I shook my head. "I just never thought of Jesus as having been a child. Now to learn that the all-powerful Son of God has a mother?"

Gaspar cocked his head, surprised that this was new information. "We call her the Blessed Mother. To be clear, she's not divine, but you should not go home without meeting her."

I stood up, handing Ezra the towel he had loaned me. "Can we meet her right away?"

"I should head home soon, but I want to see what she's like," Jacob said.

"Right, right, right. I will take you to her now. Ezra, would you please put the mirror in a safe place?"

Gaspar led Jacob and me outside, past the water storage tank to the house next door. He knocked, and I put my finger in the splintered door frame which was stained with blood from previous Passovers. The Messiah was supposed to save us on Passover. Then why didn't Jesus save us? Or Himself?

The door opened and just like that we were face-to-face with Jesus's mother.

She smiled at each of us individually. "Peace be upon you."

Gaspar took off his turban, kneeled down, and kissed the hem of her dress. That seemed like an odd greeting for someone I just met. Instead, I returned her greeting and bowed.

The tips of her sandals peeked out beneath her long, flowing dress. It was just a simple garment made of cream-colored fabric without embroidery, like any woman would wear, but somehow she looked noble. She wasn't intimidating because her demeanor was humble.

Treasure hunters have an instinct for authenticity (my recent errors in judgment notwithstanding), and there was no doubt that she was genuine. Her slender face radiated goodness.

Gaspar bowed slightly. "I am humbled that you are wearing the veil I gave you."

She touched the edge of the silvery-blue veil. "It's too beautiful to wear every day, but since you're leaving soon, I wanted you to see how much I appreciate it." Slight crinkles rested at the corners of her eyes when she smiled. "Please come in."

As we walked in, Gaspar introduced us, then said, "Eli traveled from Galilee and had hoped to meet Jesus."

Jacob quickly added, "But this morning Malachi told him Jesus had been killed."

Did Jacob have to point out the fact that I was the last person in Israel to know? My face grew hot. At least he left out the part about my being thrown into the Valley of Hinnom.

She stepped back and put her hand on her chest. "I'm sorry you had to find out that way."

"I know what Isaiah had predicted about the suffering Savior but didn't think it would happen so soon," I said. If only I could close my imagination, so I'd stop seeing Him suffer on the cross.

Gaspar shook his head. "Three years. Three years to go from an unknown man to a wanted man. But the Blessed Mother has a way of making everyone feel better." He turned toward the door. "I will leave you in good hands and return later."

She thanked him, then pulled out two cushions beneath a low table and invited us to sit down. She brought out the customary bowl for washing guests' feet. "Let me also get you something to drink." When she walked out, her long veil fluttered behind her. She moved energetically, not like someone in mourning.

I looked around the room for clues as to what her life was like. A stool sat in front of a loom, and on the counter some towels were in the process of being folded. Amazing things must've taken place there. Jesus had probably sat on that very cushion.

The Blessed Mother—it felt natural to call her that right away—handed us each a warm cup, and I took a sip of the frothy honey milk. Jesus might have drunk out of that very cup.

She gathered the folds of her dress and sat down across from us. For a moment, I just stared at her.

She turned toward me with sympathetic eyes, eyes the color of glowworms. "You've been through a great deal, haven't you?"

"It's nothing compared to what you and Jesus went through," I said.

She closed her eyes and put her fingers up to her temples near the shiny dark hair protruding from the sides of her veil.

Jacob interrupted whatever horrible scene she was imagining. "I heard He rose from the dead."

She opened her eyes and began to smile. "It's true. After three days, Jesus rose, completely restored to health."

Jesus conquered death? Great beard of my father! Malachi and the other murderers must've been shocked. What better vindication? Even Uncle Shem would have to admit that Jesus was the Son of God.

The Blessed Mother rubbed the tabletop with her fingertips. "We sat with Him right here for several wonderful meals."

"Where is Jesus right now?" I asked.

She put her hand on mine for a moment. "Oh, dear, He stayed here forty days, then ascended to heaven. Two weeks ago."

Once again, I had come so close. I forced a smile. "I'm really happy you got to see Him again." I quickly drank the last sips of my honey milk, then stared into the empty cup.

"But you're disappointed that you didn't get to meet Him?" she asked.

My voice rose a little more than I intended it to. "Even if I couldn't talk to Him, I just wanted to be in the same room with Him."

"My dear, there is far more to this than Rabbi Malachi told you." She paused. "You see, some things can only be discussed with family."

Jacob sat up straight. "You mean the family secret? I heard Longinus mention it."

"The family secret?" The Blessed Mother laughed quietly. "In a way, I guess it is."

Could the family secret have anything to do with the Ark of the Covenant? No, I wouldn't even allow myself to hope. As amazing as it was to meet His mother, even the most gentle touch couldn't change the fact that all was lost.

As I studied her, she asked, "Would the two of you consider being baptized?"

Jacob blurted out, "I've already been baptized."

"You did? When?" I asked.

"By John the Baptist. In Herod's prison."

"I'm so glad to hear that, Jacob, but this is a new rite instituted by Jesus, enabling you to become His disciple and, even more, His brother," she explained.

"His brother? I didn't even know that was possible," I said.

"Jesus's redemption made it possible. Have you ever seen your sister or mother ill and wished you could take her place instead?" she asked.

I nodded. I had wished it every day for eight weeks.

She continued, "Jesus did that. He took all the punishment we deserve and offered it to the Father on our behalf."

I was grateful that she didn't say anything for a moment as my mind tried to process Jesus's death and resurrection, so contrary to what I expected—to what we all expected.

Sometimes our lives are changed forever by a series of events that happen to us over a period of days to years, and sometimes our lives are changed forever in the tiny instant it takes for a new thought to come into our minds. Both kinds of change were happening to me, but the second kind had an even bigger impact.

Jesus did save us.

Once that revelation broke through to my mind and heart, I knew everything was different now. Not just for me, or for Jacob, or for Longinus, or even for Timon. Jesus isn't just the Redeemer for *us*, but for the whole world.

Suddenly, everything made sense, even things I didn't realize didn't make sense before that moment of dazzling clarity. My whole being seemed to awaken as if I'd been asleep all my life, waiting for that moment to wake up and realize:

Jesus did save us.

That's why He didn't save Himself! He had to make the ultimate sacrifice of His life, for all people, in order to save us. How could I have ever doubted it?

All was not lost. Though I couldn't meet Jesus, He left a legacy, and I could be part of it. "I'd like to become His disciple and brother," I said.

Jacob stood up. "And then learn the family secret."

Someone knocked on the door of an adjoining room, and the Blessed Mother called out, "Please come in."

A young, bearded man came in, carrying two chalices. "I'm sorry to disturb you. I can come back later." His Galilean accent made me a little homesick.

"I was just going to come and get you, John. Would you please baptize Eli and Jacob?"

"I'd be happy to, but we'll have to go to the western mikveh because I just heard the southern mikveh has been contaminated."

I felt Jacob's eyes piercing me, but I didn't dare look at him.

CHAPTER 26

INITIATION

Jerusalem looked better from my vantage point between John and the Blessed Mother. There were still good Israelites in the city. As we walked to the western mikveh, the Blessed Mother recommended that Jacob and I use the time to examine our consciences and repent of our sins.

I silently compared my actions to the commandments of the Torah, not all 613, of course. Why did I lie to Jacob about my bag containing the bones of my grandfather? I should've returned the gem right away. I had also been impatient and judgmental. While I was pretty good at controlling my words and actions, my thoughts often ran wild like a wheel coming off a chariot, especially thoughts about Uncle Shem.

When we reached the mikveh, John explained the Baptismal ceremony and recited some prayers. Jacob and I bowed our heads, imitating the Blessed Mother. I was surprised when John walked over and breathed on me.

I backed up a little, but the Blessed Mother whispered, "That is to exorcise unclean spirits."

I must've looked worried because she leaned in and said, "That is the custom for everyone."

John did the same thing to Jacob, then asked me to follow him into the mikveh. Inside the changing room, I hung up my tunic and went through the door to the pool room, noting that the smell of spoiled milk even emanated from my inner garments. As I descended the first slippery step, I palmed the damp wall to balance. I could practically stretch my arms and touch both side walls at once. At the second step, the cold water lapped my ankles. The sturdy roof didn't invite the sun in to warm the water. Light streamed through the openings under the roof, making it appear that the wall painting of the seven-branched candlestick was giving off candlelight. I met John in the middle of the pool.

He asked, "Eli, do you wish to be baptized?"

I suppose he had to make sure I was there by choice. "I do," I replied through chattering teeth. Two short words and I was on my way to being reconciled to God. My part was so easy because Jesus had done the painstaking work for me.

John asked, "Do you believe in God, the Father Almighty?"

After I responded, "I believe," John gently placed his palm on my head to signify that I needed to go under water. When I came out of the water, he asked me to confirm my belief in Jesus. I did, then submerged again. I came back up, took a breath, and acknowledged my belief in the Holy Spirit.

I sank down one last time and when I came up, John said, "I baptize you in the name of the Father, and of the Son, and of the Holy Spirit." He placed oil on my forehead, recited another prayer, and then concluded with, "Go in peace and may the Lord be with you."

My *amen* echoed off the stone walls. We went up the stairs, and John handed me a towel.

Just outside the door, Jacob stood there grinning, probably thinking of the last time I exited a mikveh.

The Blessed Mother surprised me with a hug. I accidentally stepped on her toes and my arm brushed against her cheek. Her skin felt as soft as an ostrich feather. I thanked her and John, now my mother and brother in Christ.

After John and Jacob went into the mikveh, she handed me a white baptismal tunic, so I took it into the changing room. The new tunic was pristine and made for a man. I pulled hard on the ends of my rope belt to tighten the large waist. My old tunic was an ugly patchwork of green, black, and orange stains, with fraying seams. I rolled it up and stuffed it in my bag.

When I came out, Jacob and John emerged from the other side. After Jacob changed, the Blessed Mother and I walked back along the ridge overlooking the Tyropean Valley, and Jacob and John followed us. One of the limestone houses had cracked down the middle, and half of it had fallen down the hillside. "Is that due to the earthquake?" I asked the Blessed Mother.

Jacob answered, "Imagine the poor owners. They're locked in their house because it's the middle of the day and the sky is darker than onyx, then their house starts shaking and sliding down the hill."

"It was dark in the middle of the day?" I asked.

"For three hours while Jesus was on the cross," Jacob said.

"Then the earthquake happened at the moment He died," John added. "It was as if the dense ground shook the people to make them realize what they had done to God."

That was the day I had fallen asleep in the shop before lunch, and when the earthquake woke me up, the room was completely dark. I figured I had slept until nighttime, but it was only midafternoon. Uncle Shem never explained what happened. Did he know that it was nature's violent reaction to the death of Jesus?

The Blessed Mother said, "Thousands of people have already repented. His death was not in vain." I looked at her and was unable to detect even a hint of bitterness.

To her left, way down in the valley, a workman bent over and loaded stones into a cart while another man stood nearby, watching and gesturing for him to hurry up. The man who was overseeing the work looked up at us, shielded his eyes from the sun with his purple sleeve, then dropped his hand onto the striped border of his cloak in disbelief. It was Malachi.

Surely, his intended purpose for those stones had nothing to do with rebuilding that house.

I turned around and looked at Jacob and John. Jacob's eyes asked if I had seen Malachi, and I nodded slightly and moved to the other side of the Blessed Mother, so I was closest to the ridge. She appeared to be looking far in the distance toward the Mount of Olives, not at the Pharisee below.

Malachi picked up two stones, grasped one in each hand, and ran toward the base of the hill. His retired muscles couldn't possibly throw the stones this high.

I kept walking but put my hand on my sheath to show him I wasn't afraid. I wanted to push down the remaining walls of the house and send stones hurtling toward him. Instead, I took hold of the Blessed Mother's elbow and steered her away from the ridge, asking her to show us King David's tomb on the way home.

John jogged to catch up with us, then walked on the other side of the Blessed Mother and cast me a meaningful glance. "I see you're already familiar with the city. After we show you David's Tomb, we'd better get the Blessed Mother home to rest."

I kept looking over my shoulder. Jacob stood on the ridge, striking his best *David versus Goliath* pose.

Leave it to Jacob to do it to a Pharisee. After launching his imaginary stone, he raised his hands victoriously and ran to catch up with us.

I remembered what Malachi had said about Jacob, "Let him go. He's not one of them." The oily cross on our foreheads and the baptismal tunics proclaimed that now both he and I were *one of them*.

CHAPTER 27

SKEPTICAL

We arrived back in the empty yard of the Blessed Mother's house and she said, "Now I can tell you the so-called family secret." She motioned for Jacob and me to sit down on the front of a wagon while she and John sat across from us on the exterior steps to the second floor of the house.

I jumped up and sat in the wagon. Since no donkeys were hitched to it, the ends of the two hitching poles rested on the ground, angling up to the front of the wagon. Jacob put one foot in front of the other and slowly walked up the incline of one of the poles, putting his arms out to balance. Apparently, he was not in any hurry to hear the secret. I had only been baptized a short time, and my patience was already being tested. Jacob made it halfway up the poles, then jumped the rest of the way and sat next to me.

The Blessed Mother clasped her hands in front of her. "John, can you please tell them Jesus's final words before He ascended?"

"First, He instructed us to make disciples of all nations, baptizing them and teaching them to observe His commands. Then He said, 'I will be with you until the end of the age.' "

Jacob raised his eyebrows. "Wait. He promised He'd be with us, then He immediately ascended to heaven?"

The Blessed Mother's eyes sparkled. "Oh, yes. He had a brilliant plan. The night before Jesus died, we celebrated the Passover feast. After Jesus prayed the blessing, He broke the bread and gave it to the disciples, saying, 'This is My Body which is given for you.' At that moment, He changed the substance of the bread into His Body.

"Then Jesus took the cup, blessed it, and said, 'This cup which is poured out for you is the New Covenant in My Blood,' and He changed the substance of wine into His Blood. He was offering Himself as the Lamb of the new Passover sacrifice."

I was grateful she paused for a moment. My mind was like Mount Vesuvius, that volcano near Rome. Some people predicted it would erupt soon, although my uncle called those people alarmists. My bedrock principles were melting, and confusion was rising with each new revelation. Jesus instituted a New Covenant? He changed bread into His Body? He ascended but promised to stay with us? I exhaled, slowly releasing some pressure.

Though no one else was around, the Blessed Mother lowered her voice. "But that was only the beginning. Before He ascended, Jesus instructed the Apostles to offer this sacrifice in memory of Him. When an Apostle represents Jesus at the sacrifice, he repeats His words, 'This is My Body which is given for you,' and at that moment the Holy Spirit changes the bread into Jesus."

The wagon was shaking because Jacob was bouncing his foot, eager to ask questions, but she continued, "Next the Apostle repeats Jesus's words, 'This cup which is poured out for you is the New Covenant in My Blood,' and the Holy Spirit changes the wine into His Precious Blood. This happens at every sacrifice.

So, you see, we still get to be with Jesus quite often."
She sat back and waited for our response.

Jacob and I looked at one another, and his reaction mirrored mine. His eyes were open wide and his mouth was open wider. He turned to the Blessed Mother. "You mean you can see Jesus on the altar?"

"We can't see Him the way He looked when He walked on the earth, but It is truly Him. It just looks like bread," she explained.

I looked at John. "But when you repeat His words, can you see Him?"

"No, the Consecrated Bread still looks exactly the same."

"But It is our Jesus—fully alive—with feet that walked miles to heal lepers, hands that healed blind men, and a face that converted sinners," she said.

"Can you see anything happening as the bread is changing into Jesus?" I asked.

John shook his head. "There's no visible sign. In fact, if an unbeliever walked into the room, he would have no idea that a miracle is taking place."

"So, you think Jesus is there? On the altar? In the bread?" Jacob asked.

"It's no longer bread," John said. "Jesus is there, just as real as when He sat inside at the table. In fact, He once told us, 'The bread that I will give is My Flesh for the life of the world.' "

There was a long pause and the only thing I could say was, "Hmm." I hated that my responses sounded like things Uncle Shem would say. Finally, I broke the silence. "How is it possible that bread is turned into Jesus?"

"It happens through the power of Jesus's words and the Holy Spirit. It's a mystery that we will never fully understand, but we accept with faith," John said.

"We call this new Passover sacrifice the Breaking of Bread, and it's how we renew Jesus's sacrifice on the cross," she added.

"Will you have it every year like Passover? I mean the old Passover?" I asked.

"Actually, we have it every single day." Her voice was full of amazement, although she had probably explained this to many pilgrims in the last few weeks. "You're both welcome to attend this evening."

It didn't seem right to attend when I was skeptical about what was happening. "It's not that I don't trust you . . ." I paused. "John, at first was it hard for you to believe that bread changes into Jesus?"

"No, because I heard it right from Jesus Himself. He testified, 'My Flesh is true food and My Blood is true drink,' and I never doubted. But it was hard for some other disciples to believe."

My reply came out shakily. "So, can I still be His follower if I don't accept this teaching?"

The Blessed Mother and John exchanged a concerned look, but his voice was gentle. "Jesus declared that unless you eat His Flesh and drink His Blood, you have no life in you."

The Blessed Mother added, "Jesus also told us that if we eat His Flesh and drink His Blood, He will abide with us and we'll have eternal life."

I felt as though I had suddenly been adopted by a foreign family. The family was very kind, of course, but I had to accept new clothes, new traditions, new food that was no longer food, and basically a new religion. I cleared my throat. "I definitely want Him to be with me and to have eternal life, but . . ." I looked at Jacob for help.

Jacob wrinkled his nose. "It just seems strange to eat Jesus."

"It helps that Jesus's humanity and divinity is hidden under the appearance and taste of bread," John said.

"Don't think of it as eating so much as welcoming Him to be closer to you than He's ever been." The Blessed Mother stood up and smiled. "This is going to take time to grasp. In the meantime, we'll leave you alone while we go make preparations for the Breaking of Bread."

John started to go up the stairs. "We'll be happy to answer more questions later. The best thing to do is ask the Holy Spirit for discernment. Now that you've been baptized, the Holy Spirit will help you understand many things."

As I leaned forward, my baptismal tunic tightened around my neck. "What if I never know for certain?"

The Blessed Mother slowly walked toward me and put her hand on my shoulder. "You don't have to know for certain. Belief without certainty is faith."

CHAPTER 28

IF HE SAYS SO

had learned the family secret, but wasn't sure that I could be part of the family. I silently prayed, *Holy Spirit, please help me to know the truth. I want to accept that the bread is changed into Jesus's Body and the wine into His Blood, but I just don't know.*

Jacob and I started walking away, so we could talk candidly. As we went under the aqueduct, cold water dripped onto my forehead. I wiped it away before it rolled to my nose. All my life, other people had made decisions for me, but now I had to decide for myself. "What do you think?" I asked.

He held out his palm. "I think it's raining."

"I mean about what the Blessed Mother and John just told us. That was a lot to absorb," I said. "If only there was a sign when the bread changed into Jesus, such as a flash of lightning or the voice of God, this would be so much easier."

"Yes, if a miracle occurs but the before-and-after looks exactly the same, how can you know for sure? Where's the proof?"

I thought about that for a minute. "On the other hand, I believed that Jesus was the Messiah without having proof. I never witnessed a miracle. I just trusted the words of friends from the synagogue who realized Jesus matched the description of the promised Messiah."

In the distance, I could see the white walls of the three-story Tower of Light. From there, a priest would blow a horn to announce the beginning and end of Sabbath. The tower reminded me of Papa. What would he have thought about all this? Papa always suggested that when you test new information for validity, it's wise to see how it fits with the facts you already know to be true.

What did I know about the expectations of the Messiah? The Messiah was supposed to give us miraculous bread from heaven. Could this bread from heaven be more than just the loaves that Jesus had multiplied? Somehow a verse I had learned in school came to mind:

THE MESSIAH WILL BEGIN TO BE REVEALED, AND THOSE WHO ARE HUNGRY WILL ENJOY THEMSELVES. AND THEY WILL MOREOVER SEE MARVELS EVERY DAY. MANNA WILL COME DOWN AGAIN, AND THEY WILL EAT OF IT.

That alluded to the miracle of the bread changing into Jesus at the daily sacrifice.

Then I reviewed what John and the Blessed Mother had told me to see if it aligned with what the prophets wrote in the Nevi'im. Jeremiah predicted that the Messiah would make a New Covenant. According to the Blessed Mother, Jesus made this New Covenant, and He did so on Passover just as we expected.

Isaiah said that the Messiah's name would be Immanuel, which means God is with us. Although Jesus ascended, He said He'd be with us if we eat His Flesh. Wasn't it just like God to figure out a way for His Son to be with us even after He had risen? Sure enough, John and the Blessed Mother's explanations were consistent with everything I had learned.

I thought we had been walking aimlessly until Jacob stopped outside the circus.

A Roman was standing at the arched entrance. "The chariot race is starting now. I have a few tickets left." He studied us from head to toe. "Are you followers of Jesus?"

"How did you know? Oh, our baptismal tunics," I said.

The dark red feathers in his helmet swayed as he nodded. "He was a righteous man. Righteous."

"We never got to meet Him," I said.

"But we met His mother and His Apostle, and they're very kind," Jacob added.

Jacob was right. The Blessed Mother and John were completely trustworthy. So why couldn't I just hurry up and believe them? Then it occurred to me. I didn't have to believe *them*.

I just had to believe *Him:* Jesus.

There was no doubt that Jesus was the Messiah, so if He said, "This is My Body," He wouldn't lie. If He said it was true, then it was true. Suddenly I had no more doubts.

I motioned for Jacob to follow me a few feet away, so the Roman couldn't hear us. I stood beside a huge bronze statue of Apollo in his chariot, holding the reins of four rearing horses in one hand and a whip in the other. I pointed at it. "I've never seen this before."

Jacob ran his fingers along the grooves in one horse's tail. "It's new. So life-like."

I shook my head. "Apollo in Jerusalem? It's worse than the golden calf. The people won't stand for this. Anyway, what I wanted to tell you is—"

Right then, the horn blew to signal the start of the chariot race.

When it finally finished, my words came rushing out. "I'm going back to attend the Breaking of Bread." I grinned and waited for his reply.

He leaned back on the wheel of Apollo's chariot. "Huh. So, you believe it?"

"Without a doubt. Do you?" I asked.

He folded his hands and put them up to his lips. He didn't say anything for a moment, then he put his hands down and started to nod. "I do."

"Hurry. Let's go," I said, striding away. "I can't believe I'm going to be in the same room as Jesus." I didn't hear Jacob's heavy footsteps behind me, so I turned around.

He stood up but didn't move. "Let's go after the chariot race."

I jogged back to him. "I've been waiting to meet Jesus for so long."

"And we will. Tomorrow." He took coins out of his bag. "I'll even pay for your ticket."

"Jacob, I'm going back now." I lowered my voice. "The Son of God is going to be in that room. Don't you want to be there?"

The coins jingled in his hand as he shifted from one leg to the other. "God is present everywhere."

"His Spirit is everywhere, but this is different. If we had gotten here two weeks ago, and you knew Jesus was going to be there for supper, would you have gone?"

"Of course," he said.

"It's the same Jesus. He is going to be there. That's the only place in the world where He'll be physically present." I looked Jacob squarely in the eye, but like Apollo, his gaze was fixed on the bronze horses.

Then he looked over his shoulder toward the circus, and back at me. He shrugged, walked to the Roman, and paid for his ticket. "I'll meet you there tomorrow."

I replied with his favorite phrase, "If you say so."

He was about to go in when he turned around.

I hoped he had changed his mind.

Instead, he said, "If I miss you somehow, stop by our house on your way back to Galilee."

As the announcer's booming voice welcomed spectators, Jacob of Jericho, the future world-famous charioteer, walked through the circus entrance. I doubted I would ever see him again.

CHAPTER 29

ENCOUNTER

I ran the entire way back to the Blessed Mother, and she must've heard me coming because she met me at the door. My words pushed their way through heaving breaths. "I believe. I really believe that the bread changes into Jesus."

She glanced at the sky, then back at me. "Already? Praise be to the Holy Spirit for revealing these things to you. It didn't take you long."

"It's not hard to believe something when the Son of God says it's so," I said.

"Very true." She looked over my head to the street. But Jacob wasn't there. She bit her lower lip while her eyes searched left toward the other neighbor's house and right toward Ezra's.

Should I have tried to explain why Jacob wasn't there? She didn't ask. She smiled and welcomed me into the house.

John was sitting at the table reading a scroll. He greeted me and I looked at him in awe. Humble, soft-spoken John was able to stand in Jesus's place and help bring about a miracle.

"You've waited long enough, Eli," she said. "We'll take you to Jesus right now before the Breaking of Bread."

"Where?" I asked, trying to look through two open doors into the adjoining rooms.

"Yesterday the bread was changed into Jesus. We call Him in this form the Blessed Sacrament, and He remains in the tabernacle in the Upper Room," she said.

I had been in the same house with Jesus and hadn't even known it. "Are you sure I'm ready to be in His Presence?"

"I assure you, your soul has never been so radiant." She put her arm around my shoulders and guided me toward the Upper Room. "He has been waiting for you."

John went ahead of us and unlocked the door. As he opened it, I spotted the rectangular gold tabernacle on the altar. Before moving any further, the Blessed Mother and John genuflected, so I kept my eyes on the tabernacle and did the same. We walked to the front of the room, passing rows of wooden benches. Next to the first row, we kneeled and bowed low.

Then John stood up and walked to the tabernacle. I kept bowing but lifted my head, so I could watch. He pushed aside the purple veil. My reverent posture was veiling my excitement. A little leaked out when I smiled. John opened the tabernacle, removed the Blessed Sacrament, and placed It in a shiny silver holder.

I looked at what appeared to be regular unleavened Passover bread. *Jesus! My Lord and King!* The words resounded from the depths of my soul, but I muzzled them before they became audible.

I've looked forward to meeting You for so long. Thank You for this great gift of being in Your Presence. A few hours ago, I was excited just to touch a cup and a cushion that You touched, but now here I am sitting so close to You.

I continued talking to Him silently. *Thank You for Your providence during my journey. For rescuing me from Hinnom and helping me deliver the mirror on time. And for letting me meet John and Your mother.*

The Blessed Mother was kneeling with her head tilted, a sweet smile on her lips, and absolute love in her eyes. John was lying on the floor with his arms stretched out, his body forming the shape of a cross.

I imagined the two of them standing on Calvary, watching helplessly as Jesus hung on the cross, struggling to breathe. I looked at Jesus and said, *It's a shame the world didn't love You the way You deserve to be loved. I'm sorry You endured all that torture, but I'm grateful You were willing to be my Redeemer. I pray that all of Israel and the world will come to believe in You and discover Your Divine Presence.*

The shiny holder for the Blessed Sacrament was about a foot tall and embellished with chubby angel faces and small emeralds, rubies, and sapphires. Whoever crafted it was skilled with the planishing hammer.

Then I realized my mind had started to wander, so I returned my gaze to Jesus. *Please help Uncle Shem come to believe that You're the Messiah, and let Mama meet You someday too. Let Jacob come to You tomorrow. And please heal Tamar.*

I retrieved my prayer list from all the other lists in the treasure chest of my imagination, and asked Him to help everyone on that list. I put the scroll back and paused a moment. The bottom of my imaginary treasure chest had a false floor. Underneath it is where I hid one particular scroll. On the outside of the wrinkled paper, I had scrawled the words *Taxes Paid Each Year,* a title that wouldn't stir anybody's curiosity.

Written on the inside was the list of all the things I worried about. There were a few old things on the list like would we be able to keep our home, which I wrote right after Papa died. I mentally crossed off a few things and thanked Jesus for helping with them. Then I decided to tell Him about all my other worries: that Uncle Shem might not be treating Mama well while I was gone, how I was dreading going home to be his apprentice, that I could never please him, and on and on. I explained everything without even pausing to think about what I would say, or how I should say it.

When I was finished, I sat back on my heels for a minute. I imagined myself standing up and putting that scroll beside the tabernacle, then leaving it there. As long as I could visit Jesus, I no longer needed the false floor in my imaginary treasure chest.

I felt like Abel, talking so much, so I kneeled again and just enjoyed being in His Presence. Sometime later, John stood up, placed the Blessed Sacrament back in the tabernacle, closed the door, and moved the veil in front of it.

I inhaled the scent of burning candles and incense, then exhaled slowly. We walked to the door, then kneeled and faced the tabernacle once more. We stayed that way for several moments, not wanting to leave until the Blessed Mother finally stood up. At the threshold of the holiest room on earth, I turned and stole a final glance at the veiled Divine Presence.

While the Blessed Mother went back to folding the towels, John invited me to greet the other disciples gathering for the Breaking of Bread.

Outside in the yard, I spotted a familiar face in a small group of people. Despite his tidy appearance, the scar above his eyebrow confirmed his identity. It was Timon, the former bandit who had given me his dagger.

As I approached Timon's group of friends, one of them said, "There's talk that the Apostles will soon be arrested."

Timon put his hands on his hips, inadvertently pushing back his cloak and revealing that he no longer had a sheath attached to his belt. "Isn't it ironic that I've converted, yet I'm still on the wrong side of the law? I know I'm on the right side, though, and I'll help them any way I can."

I couldn't wait to tell Timon how his dagger helped me avoid being kidnapped by his bandit friends.

He looked over his shoulder and noticed me standing behind him. "Eli, you made it!"

"I arrived this morning," I said.

Timon's eyes darted to the other groups of people gathered in the yard. "Your mother?"

"She's well but not strong enough to make the journey."

"I'm glad she's well. When I met Jesus, I asked Him to heal her," he said.

I had been praying to God for Mama's healing, but to know that Jesus was personally involved somehow surprised me. "Well, He did. Thank you for remembering. So, you got to spend time with Jesus?"

"I was with Him for a few weeks before He ascended. Since then I have been with Him in the Breaking of Bread."

From the staircase, John announced that all the disciples could come in for the sacrifice, so the people lowered their voices and headed toward the outside steps.

I whispered to Timon, "Let's talk afterwards. There's something I want to tell you."

He raised his eyebrows. "Is it about your uncle? I've been anxious for you to learn the truth."

CHAPTER 30

THE ARK OF THE *NEW* COVENANT

hat do you mean, 'the truth about my uncle?' I was just going to tell you how your dagger saved me," I said to Timon. Beads of sweat formed on his forehead.

"Back at our house, you called him foolish. Why?" I asked.

He wiped the sweat off his forehead with the end of his cloak. "Uh . . . you see . . . we better be quiet now." He raced up the steps for the Breaking of Bread.

Why was he more nervous than a lamb on Passover? I'd have to wait for the answer.

The Blessed Mother stood outside the Upper Room, letting everyone go ahead of her. Timon motioned for her to go ahead of us, and she gave him a grateful smile.

When it was our turn to enter the room, my eyes locked on the tabernacle, and I genuflected, silently saying, *My Lord and my God.*

On each side of the room, ten benches were lined up, each having enough space for about five people, though most were crammed with more. We followed the Blessed Mother to the second bench on the left, and three young girls moved to the end to make room for us.

Gaspar, no longer wearing his turban, sat across the main aisle with the men from his caravan. One of them waved at me.

I slowly raised my hand in greeting, then realized it was the Persian who had come to my village months ago and asked to buy a mirror—a mirror intended for Gaspar's sister!

Everyone prayed for several minutes, and I tried to see the tabernacle, but a tall man kneeled in front of me, blocking my view, so I scooted to the right, banging into Timon's bicep.

John processed up the aisle and another man followed him. I assumed he was Peter based on what John had told me. Everyone stood up and sang a hymn, and the Blessed Mother's sweet voice contrasted with Timon's raspy one, but both were sincere.

The first part of the sacrifice was very similar to a synagogue service, but this was much more exciting because soon a miracle would take place. They recited a prayer which I recognized from the Hallel psalm we always sang on Passover.

Then Peter explained how Jesus fulfilled the prophets' predictions about the Messiah. At the end, he quoted Isaiah, who said that when salvation came, God would also call the outcasts of Israel to form the assembly.

Timon elbowed me in the ribs, pointed to himself, and whispered, "Outcast." We chuckled and there was a rustling sound as many other people looked at one another and smiled, recognizing themselves as redeemed outcasts.

While the people sang a psalm, John went to the end of the aisle to meet the men bringing up unleavened bread, a jug, a chalice, and baskets with offerings for the poor. That meant the miracle was about to happen.

After the assembly kneeled, Peter continued praying, then moved his hands over the unleavened bread. The room was silent except for the tinkling of a small bell. Peter bowed low over the bread and repeated Jesus's words.

I didn't move a muscle. At that moment the Holy Spirit changed the bread into Jesus. There was no glowing light shining down on His Presence, no voice from heaven, but I knew it happened. And I was only twelve feet away from the miracle.

Peter genuflected, then stood up, holding the Consecrated Host high for everyone to adore. While the Blessed Mother bowed low, I silently prayed, *My Lord, I know It is really You and I praise You.*

Then Peter prayed over the chalice. After genuflecting, he held the chalice up high and I interiorly said, *Jesus, blessed be Your Holy Blood.*

The man in front of me walked out to the aisle with folded hands. Though he wasn't wearing his soldier's uniform, it was definitely Longinus. He was deep in prayer and didn't notice me. Who would've thought? Even a Roman was a redeemed outcast.

Timon stood up, but I wasn't sure what to do. I started to stand but froze until the Blessed Mother nodded and stood as well. Since she was behind me, vouching for me in a way, I felt more acceptable to Jesus. I followed Timon to the front of the room, then kneeled and awaited the Bread from Heaven. My heart was beating so loudly that I looked at Timon to see if he could hear it. He was focused on Jesus between Peter's fingers.

As Peter stood before me and lifted the Sacred Host, I silently said, *Jesus, I know It is You.* Peter placed the Sacred Host in my palm, and I put It in my mouth, praying, *Jesus, You are welcome here.* John offered me the chalice of Jesus's Blood and I took a sip, then glided back to my bench with the Redeemer inside of me, His mother behind me, a converted bandit in front of me, and outcasts all around me. The congregation was a showcase of some of God's best work.

I kneeled down back at our bench. *Jesus, thank You for letting me participate in Your New Sacrifice. I guess Mama's right. I need to be grateful for Your mercy as well as Your justice. By this Sacred Host, would You make me more like You? I admire Your courage and strength. Help me to do Your will.* Then I decided to be quiet and give Him a chance to talk to me. I didn't hear Him say anything, but perhaps my soul did and would remember it later.

Peter placed the chalice with the remaining Sacred Hosts in the tabernacle, closed the door, and moved the veil in front of it. Jesus was present behind that veil just as the Ark of the Covenant and the Divine Presence had been behind the veil in the Holy of Holies in the Temple.

The hair on my arms stood up, a sign that my treasure-hunting instincts were activated. I realized that we didn't need the Ark of the Covenant anymore. We had found the Divine Presence, the greatest Treasure on earth, a hidden Treasure that not everybody could find. I was the most fortunate treasure hunter ever.

I began to mentally retrieve my list of found treasures so I could add Him to the list, but I stopped and abruptly put it back. A word on a scroll in an imaginary treasure chest wasn't necessary. I had just become a tabernacle for the Treasure Itself and I would never forget it.

CHAPTER 31

A VISION FROM JESUS'S VANTAGE POINT

fter the Breaking of Bread, Timon wasn't around to answer my question, but Longinus was outside, and I had a question for him too. He was standing alone in the yard, just a few feet from the mud puddle I had created under the water tank earlier that day.

"I hardly recognized you in your new tunic," he said.

"I hardly recognized you without your uniform. Why didn't you tell me you're a follower of Jesus?" I asked.

"The truth about Jesus's Real Presence is hard enough to accept. Coming from a Roman, it would've sounded like a myth."

"I suppose," I said.

Then John walked over and greeted us. "Eli, do you have a place to stay tonight?"

"I haven't thought about it. I guess I could see if there's room at Ezra's inn."

"Please stay here with us," he replied.

We spoke to Longinus for a bit longer, then headed inside. John put out a sleeping mat in his room on the first floor, and I would've fallen asleep immediately, but he was gathering traveling supplies, preparing to take Jesus to other lands.

I lay there and reflected on the day that seemed to last half my life. It was hard to believe that just that morning I had found out Jesus had been killed. Within hours, I was under the same roof as He was. Throughout the night, I smiled whenever I rolled over.

The next morning Gaspar came over, and we talked about our journeys to Jerusalem. His Persian accent was so different from my Galilean accent and his voice was deep, but excitable. In fact, he would be a skilled announcer for sporting events, particularly something unpredictable like baby goat racing.

His journey had been longer, but less harrowing because he traveled with a caravan. He invited me to ride part of the way home with them as their route went within a day's walk of my village. They planned to leave the next day.

"You live so far away. How did your grandfather know the Messiah had been born?" I asked him.

"For this, I need to show you," he said. We went out into the side yard between the house and Ezra's inn. He unrolled his star chart on the dusty ground. "Which constellation is your favorite?"

We crouched down to look. On the scroll was a dark circle intersected by straight lines to form precise wedges. Within each of the wedges were strange letters and several small Xs and triangles. "Honestly, I don't see any orderly arrangement. Treasure maps make much more sense to me," I said.

"This was a treasure map to my grandfather." He pointed to a large star on the map. "That's Jupiter. When Jesus was born, my grandfather saw an incredibly bright star. Jupiter and Venus aligned with the star Regulus in the constellation Leo."

"That was enough to make him travel this far?" I asked.

"Here's how he understood it. Jupiter is the king planet. Regulus means little king. Venus was named for the Roman goddess of love and mother-hood, and Leo, the lion constellation, symbolizes the tribe of Judah."

"But you don't worship Roman gods," I said.

"Not at all. It meant that God, the real king, re-vealed through the stars that He sent His Son through a human mother to Israel. My grandfather knew that if he followed the star, he would find the King's Son. And he did."

"It must have taken great faith for your grandfather to look at a baby and believe He was God."

He nodded. "But I think it takes even more faith to look at Consecrated Bread and realize It is God."

"That's true. He adored the Word made Flesh, and we adored the bread made Flesh."

He pointed at the Upper Room. "It's going to be hard to leave here, no?"

I sighed. "There's no place like it. Let's not think about having to leave."

"At least you come to Jerusalem three times a year for feasts," he said.

I wished there was something I could say to cheer him up. But what could he have in his palace that could compete with Jesus? Nothing.

"I wonder if the Apostles will stay here? Certain Pharisees are targeting Jesus's followers." I told him how Malachi had stolen my bag and thrown me into the Valley of Hinnom.

He shook his head sympathetically.

I explained the whole story of how I had broken Uncle Shem's first mirror and how I thought I would fail to deliver the new one. Finally, I confided about wanting to become a treasure hunter to get out of being Uncle Shem's apprentice.

When I finished, Gaspar sat back and spoke quietly. "You went to such great lengths just so I could get a novelty for my sister. I am terribly sorry."

"But if you hadn't ordered the mirror, I wouldn't have met Jesus. I'd be back in Galilee, mourning His death."

The excitement returned to his voice. "Well, now when you get home, your uncle will finally be pleased with you."

"I suppose." I looked away, studying the tops of the Roman towers in the distance. "The thing about him being pleased is that it's only a temporary condition, like being full. Give it a few hours and he'll find another reason to criticize. I'll have to keep proving myself again and again."

"Look at everything you have endured, Eli. You have shown courage, integrity, and fortitude. Do not let your uncle's opinion shape your image of yourself."

"I appreciate that, but when he starts criticizing, somehow I become Slapdash again."

"It is hard not to care what others think. Because I am part of the royal family, I hear flattery all day long." He mimicked a servant's high-pitched voice. "Gaspar, you perfect little prince, you sneezed at just the right time. Gaspar, you are so skilled at growing your hair."

I laughed loudly. "I can't imagine what that's like."

Gaspar smoothed his robe and sat up straight. "My father made sure I do not let other people's opinions influence my view of myself. He always said, 'God's opinion of you is the only one that matters.' "

I nodded. "In other words, 'We are only what we are in the eyes of God and nothing more.' "

"Right, right, right," he said.

I smirked. "You had that inscribed on your sister's mirror."

"A mirror does not lie. Even Jesus could not please everybody, and He is perfect." He looked at the sun and started rolling up his star chart. "This evening after the Breaking of Bread, we will go to the amphitheater and from that height, you will see the constellations."

I tried to savor every moment of the Breaking of Bread, not knowing if I'd ever get to participate again. After the sacrifice, John put the Blessed Sacrament out for adoration, and I moved up to the front row.

I was silently speaking to Jesus about going back to work with Uncle Shem when suddenly the room filled with incense. After the smoke cleared a little, I was looking down on my body which was kneeling about nine feet away. Was I dreaming or dying?

Above my head, a huge scroll appeared. It unrolled to the size of a blanket, revealing a picture of burning candles, sparkling mica flakes, squirming glowworms, a shining emerald, and two rushing waterfalls.

On the far left, the picture of a seven-branched candlestick was so realistic that the flames flickered and gave off enough heat to warm my scalp. Below the candlestick, I saw a vision of things that happened months ago in my home. I was carrying forty-pound bags of limestone out to the forge, then running up to prepare Mama's herbal medicine. With a whooshing sound, the flames grew until they covered the entire scene, and a cool breeze blew them out. Immediately, the candles melted to nubs and streams of wax dripped down, forming the word *capable* below the candlestick.

That scene disappeared and a ribbon of smoke drifted toward the sparkling mica flakes suspended in a swaying bubble. The bubble popped, and the mica flakes fell down into a vision of me swimming in the cave on Sabbath. I floated on my back and water swirled around my legs, causing the mica flakes at my feet to form the word *obedient*. When I kicked my feet and splashed the sparkling word, it ascended and hung in midair at the top of the scroll.

Next the glowworms' light dimmed, then brightened three times. Beneath them was a vision of me inside Tamar's cave, leaving food in her bowl, then walking away as my stomach growled. The scene disappeared except for the glowworms that curled up and formed the word *selfless*.

Next, a pyramid-shaped emerald started spinning and putting off rainbow-colored rays of light. The rays bent toward one another, forming a vision in which I saw myself place the emerald on the bucket in Jacob's stable. Then the emerald broke apart and thousands of pieces flew at me. I tried to touch them, but they receded to the top of the scroll, forming the gleaming word *honorable*.

Lastly, two rushing waterfalls met halfway down the scroll. The water slowed and became like a sheet of glass on which a scene appeared. I saw myself under the water in the western mikveh. As I came up out of the water, the waterfalls poured down onto me. Water was deflected off my shoulders to the top of the scroll where it formed large clouds that spelled the words *man of God*.

The scroll rolled up, then disappeared. The incense cleared and when I blinked, I was looking at Jesus in the Blessed Sacrament again. I realized the vision of me had been from His vantage point on the altar. He had just shown me the way I looked in His eyes. *Capable. Obedient. Selfless. Honorable. Man of God.*

I immediately bent down and touched my forehead to the cold floor, extending my arms in the shape of a cross and silently praying, *Thank You for understanding me, Jesus. Thank You for valuing me.* I didn't care who saw me. I no longer needed to worry what Uncle Shem or anyone else thought of me. God's opinion was the only one that mattered, and it was better than I ever could've imagined.

Across from me, Gaspar stepped out into the aisle, twirled his hand, bowed to the Blessed Sacrament, then kneeled for a moment. The Blessed Mother and John remained in adoration.

I followed Gaspar outside and down the exterior steps. When we reached the yard, he put his turban back on and I whispered, "You were right. I only need to care what God thinks. Being with Jesus was like being finished by a planishing hammer."

He raised his eyebrows, making the corners disappear under his turban. "That sounds like something a Pharisee would say."

"No, it's a good thing. You see, the planishing hammer removes all the marks made by other hammers and smooths the metal until you have a finely crafted piece."

"Right, right, right. The Master Craftsman planished the dents Uncle Shem made," he said.

I nodded. "And He provided a type of armor, preventing future dents." Fortunately, I put on that armor just in time.

CHAPTER 32

FOOLED

I was prepared to face the one who wielded the hammer of insults, but couldn't have imagined it would be that soon. Gaspar, Longinus, and I were on the third floor of the amphitheater just a few blocks away from the Upper Room. Through the openings framed by marble arches, we could see the sun starting to set, two stars in the sky, and the entire city down below. Gaspar was pointing out where the planet Jupiter would be. Suddenly Timon came up the steps behind us.

I turned around. "Timon! I've been looking for you."

His grumpy face looked worried. "And I've been avoiding you. Afraid I would say the wrong thing. But I thought you might need some help now."

"Why's that?" I asked.

Uncle Shem came up the steps.

I took a step back. Even the stars seemed too close.

Uncle Shem took the cloak off his head and draped it over his shoulders. "You are here."

Longinus and Gaspar stood shoulder-to-shoulder with me. "I was planning to head home in the morning. I have your money," I said.

Uncle Shem's lips widened into a fake smile. "Well, I'm glad everything went well. Ezra told me where to find you."

"Are you checking up on me?" I asked.

"No, that's not—"

"Because I did everything you asked. And it wasn't easy," I said, warning myself to stay calm and respectful.

"I'm sure—"

I interrupted him again. "You sent me on this journey knowing it was too far to walk in that amount of time."

Uncle Shem tugged on his beard but didn't say a word.

"And you didn't give me directions to Ezra's."

"Yet you figured it out," he said.

I raised my voice. "Only because a Roman helped me!" I flashed Longinus an apologetic look.

Uncle Shem stared at the floor. "Let me explain. When your mother was sick, and I heard Jesus was killed—"

"Wait. You knew before I left, and you didn't tell me?"

He rubbed his palms together, and the scratching sound of dry skin broke the silence. "I heard He died and rose again but was afraid of getting involved until I knew for sure."

I crossed my arms.

"I know, I know. It sounds despicable," he said, glancing at Timon, then back at me. "It's time you knew the truth. When you were little, I became a follower of Benji, a man who claimed to be the Messiah. I was his most enthusiastic supporter. When we discovered he was a fraud, I felt terrible for leading some devout people astray."

I uncrossed my arms. That's what Timon and Ezra had been alluding to. Who would've thought?

Uncle Shem continued, "Everybody in Israel knew I was a fool. I brought shame to our family. I lost everything, my reputation, my business, my home. If it wasn't for your parents, I would've been forced to leave Israel. I'll be forever indebted to them." He took a deep breath. "Anyway, I've been trying to rebuild my reputation ever since."

"That's why the mirror was so important to you!" I blurted out.

"When it came to Jesus, I was too concerned about what people would think of me to decide for myself. And I knew you'd find the truth at all costs," he said.

"Me? Why would you think that?"

"Because you're more prudent than I am." He extended his arm like a stiff olive branch and rested his hand on my shoulder. "I'm sorry I've been so hard on you, Eli. Things are going to be different from now on. People can change. Right, Timon?"

Timon nodded. "You bet. Bandits, outcasts, and even devout Israelites."

I studied Uncle Shem's humble stance. Were these just words, or had he really changed? Jesus would want me to forgive him, but I didn't have to put myself in a position to be hurt by him again. It would take time to rebuild trust. He needed to be perfected by the planishing hammer too. "Well, calling me Eli instead of Slapdash is a good start."

Uncle Shem blushed. "Together we can make beautiful mirrors, and you can deliver them all over Israel. I know how you like seeing new places."

I looked in the distance and considered his offer. South of the Temple over the mikveh, rain poured down from two clouds shaped like cupped hands. Though the clouds didn't form words like they did in my vision, they reminded me of my new identity as a man of God. I wasn't meant to be a metalsmith or a treasure hunter. I was meant to be a *Treasure bearer.* "Actually, I'm not going back to Galilee with you. I'm going to help the Apostles introduce Jesus to the world."

I didn't watch for Uncle Shem's reaction. Pleasing God was more important. "Can I start by introducing you to Jesus?" I asked.

He looked toward the Temple. "How? Where?"

I pointed toward the Upper Room and started to explain, but my words froze in my throat. Several blocks away, three men were striding toward the Upper Room. I squinted to see better. The shortest man turned slightly, and I recognized the silhouette of his raised chin, flowing headdress, and protruding phylactery. "Malachi!"

CHAPTER 33

FALLING INTO EVIL HANDS

My body felt heavy, as if it was being filled with molten lead. Longinus, Gaspar, and Timon turned around to look through the arches of the amphitheater. Malachi and two guards were approaching the Upper Room.

The Blessed Mother and John were in danger. And the Blessed Sacrament! "We have to go back!" I yelled.

Longinus waved his hand toward the ground. "They're blocking the street." Directly below us, a century of soldiers stood practicing a drill, clogging the entire street along the amphitheater.

I shouted, "Longinus and Timon, let's take the shortcut!"

I turned to go, but Longinus yelled after me. "Running on the wall? It's still wet from the rain!"

"Uncle Shem, Gaspar, you take the street and if you beat us there, get everybody out." I raced to the southeast side of the amphitheater, right above the city wall. I put one knee on top of the railing, then pushed my body up and over. I dropped about seven feet and landed on the wall.

I remained crouching and steadied myself. Below me, the palm tree fronds flapped in the wind, sounding like scurrying cockroaches. Under the palm tree fronds were rooftop terraces of several large homes. A few blocks down, on the street, a man looked up and pointed me out to his friend.

Timon dropped down, then Longinus. I patted my dagger to make sure it was still in my sheath and took off running along the wall. The wind blasted my body, so I leaned into it. On the left side was the ravine that led to the Lower City, which would double the drop from forty feet to eighty feet. The ground spun below.

I stared ahead, focusing on running in the center of the wall. Though the surface was wet, somehow my sandals gripped like gladiator shoes, and I made it about halfway across. Timon breathed heavily right behind me. In front of me, at the end of the wall was a Roman tower. On the balcony, a soldier stood guard, his spear leaning against the tower. To him it would look as though Longinus was chasing us.

The soldier must've heard Timon cough because he hastily picked up his spear. *"Consiste!"*

What would arrive sooner? Longinus's breathless explanation or the soldier's hasty conclusion and his spear?

I wasn't going to find out. Next to the wall was a tall house. I jumped down about ten feet and landed on the rooftop terrace. My feet smacked hard on the stone. Attached to that house was a shorter house, and together they created a stairstep. I jumped down another ten feet to the red-tiled roof. I strained to see the Upper Room, but other houses blocked my view. Timon jumped down beside me.

"Where's Longinus?" I asked.

Timon rubbed the back of his neck. "He was right behind me. You don't think he fell?"

I looked over my shoulder at the wet wall. "Surely not. He's done this before." I looked down on the ground but there was no sign of him. I walked to the edge of the roof. It was the last house in the row, so the drop to the ground would be twenty feet. I sat on the edge, ready to hang from the clay tiles.

Timon yelled from a few feet away. "Over here. There's a canopy!"

I ran to his side. The canopy on the front of the house appeared taut and strong. "I'll go first and see if it holds me." I jumped facedown, spreading my arms and legs to distribute my weight. My torso sunk into the yellow fabric and it billowed up around me. The canopy drooped but didn't break. I crawled across to the edge and jumped down the remaining ten feet.

I waited for Timon, but he yelled, "Go, go, go!"

I sprinted two blocks to Ezra's inn and peeked around the corner. Nobody was in the street. There was a horse-drawn wagon in front of the inn. The sky wasn't dark yet, but Ezra had lit the torches on both corners of his building.

I snuck past the bubbling fountain and slunk between the horses and the inn. I squatted and looked through the wagon wheel. The side yard was quiet. Something was huddled at the top of the exterior steps leading to the Upper Room. On second glance, I realized it was only a large jug.

Timon arrived and tiptoed toward me.

"Do you think Malachi's inside?" I whispered.

He nodded. "Making arrests. Let's go to the Upper Room instead of going in the front." He stood up and ran toward the exterior steps, and I followed him.

As he approached the water tank, three figures popped out from behind the wide columns. The guards rushed at Timon. I should've given him back his dagger.

Malachi was running toward me, his arm out-stretched, holding a knife. "So, you escaped the fires of Hinnom? Now you're overly confident."

I ran back to the wagon. On the floor was a horse-whip, so I grabbed it and turned around. I swung the whip at him, but it struck the ground in front of me. I tried again, but it lashed my ankle. My skin burned as blood seeped to the surface.

He cackled. "The traitor is doing our job for us."

I swung the whip harder. It hissed at the air, then scourged his hand. A bright streak of blood con-trasted his gray skin. He howled and backed away, sticking his hand up his wide sleeve.

Timon and a guard wrestled on the ground near the water tank. Timon got on top of him, clutching the guard's throat. The other guard stood behind Timon and drew back his club.

I shouted, "Behind you!"

Timon looked over his shoulder as the club whacked the back of his head. He moaned and collapsed on top of the other guard. The guard wriggled out from under him, stood up, and stomped on Timon's back. They put chains on his ankles and wrists, then dragged him to the bottom of the steps.

Malachi inched closer to me. He palmed the knife while blood dripped down his wrist.

As I pulled the whip back over my head, it snagged on a nail protruding from the roof overhang. I yanked on it, but it wouldn't budge. I left it hanging from the roof.

I ran into the back of the wagon and crouched next to the sideboard. It was just a retreat, not a surrender. I peeked through a crack in the wood.

Malachi turned around and yelled at the guard. "Bar the front door! No one gets out."

Just then, Gaspar came up and hid between the wagon and Ezra's inn. His turban was gone, and his dark eyes were wide. He whispered, "Did the Blessed Mother get out?"

I looked toward the Upper Room. "I think . . ." My voice cracked. "I think she's still in there."

Gaspar bolted across the yard. Malachi grabbed his golden belt, but the silky fabric slipped out of his hand. Gaspar started up the stairs to the Upper Room. The guards left their post at the front door and chased him. He was halfway up when a guard reached between the railings and grabbed his foot. Gaspar crashed down onto his hands and knees.

The other guard raced up the steps and scooped him up. He dropped Gaspar onto the landing and started to tie him to the railing.

Gaspar shouted, "Your evil plan will not work, Malachi! Stop them, Eli!"

Malachi yelled, "Put him inside!"

The guard tied Gaspar's hands and legs, then shoved him in the Upper Room.

Malachi spoke between clenched teeth. "Now barricade the door."

The guard reached into his bag and brought out two gladiator shoes.

I winced.

He threw one gladiator shoe down to the guard standing at the bottom of the steps, who was smart enough not to try to catch it. It landed on the ground in front of Timon's head, probably leaving a spiky footprint. That guard carried it to the front door while the first guard lodged a shoe under the door to the Upper Room.

I had to do something. Since I was outnumbered, my only chance was wits, not violence. I looked up and prayed for help. Above me a rope was strung from a hook on Ezra's wall to the hatch door of the water tank. I took out Timon's dagger and started to saw the end of the rope that was attached to the wall. Malachi and the guard were still adjusting the gladiator shoe under the front door.

My blade gnawed at the rope fibers. At first they held firm, but one after another they started to sever. Finally, the end of the rope broke free, and I tied it to the back of the wagon. It hung a little lower than when it was attached to the wall, but wasn't noticeably different.

Malachi walked from the front door toward me. "Come out, heathen." When he was close enough to touch the wagon, he grabbed the torch from Ezra's wall. "Forget the arrests. We'll just burn the entire house." The flames sizzled as he waved the torch in the air. "And everyone in it."

I swallowed hard. The front door of the Blessed Mother's house opened but only an inch. The gladiator shoe held firm. A hand grasped the edge of the door. The only thing that escaped was a piercing scream.

The houses were so close together. If one house burned, the entire row would be consumed.

The door to the Upper Room opened a crack, and Gaspar's fingers reached around the door. Who was in there with him?

I stood up in the back of the wagon and brandished the dagger.

Malachi looked up at me, then kept stepping back. The guards rushed to his side.

I had one opportunity. I had to be precise.

His eyes darted left and right. The light from the torch reflected onto the bottom of the water tank. "Throw it. You'll only hit one of us. Your friends will still burn."

I took aim. "That mikveh didn't clean your soul. In fact, I think it would take a flood." I threw the dagger. It whizzed by him, coming close enough to knock the smugness right off his face. It clanged on a hitching post behind him.

Just as I hoped, the loud noise spooked the horses, and they began galloping away. I grasped the reins but looked over my shoulder. The rope going from the back of the wagon to the hatch door on the tank was getting pulled tight as the wagon sped off. The water tank started to shake. Malachi looked up just as the force pulled the hatch door open, then completely ripped it off. A wall of water poured onto him and the guards, slamming them to the ground.

A narrow escape aided by a crashing wall of water—my own Exodus!

CHAPTER 34

GLORIOUS RETURN

f only Jacob could have seen how much I looked like a charioteer! My legs were bent and my feet were planted as I leaned back, pulling firmly on the reins as the spooked horses pulled the careering wagon down the empty street. My hair was blown up, probably resembling the feathers on a Roman helmet. My tunic bulged out behind me. The wind whipped my face but couldn't erase the grin spread across it. I yelled, "Great beard of my father! Justice!"

The two men who had seen me running on the wall began to walk out into the street but stepped back clumsily right before the wagon sped past. Behind the wagon, the rope was being dragged through the dirt, and at the end the hatch door bounced on the ground. The horses circled David's Tomb and started to trot as we headed back to the Upper Room.

I parked outside and dislodged the gladiator shoe from underneath the front door. Two little girls ran out, followed by the Blessed Mother, Gaspar, and Longinus.

The Blessed Mother rushed over to me. "Eli, you're safe!"

"I thought you and John were in the Upper Room," I said.

"John was until Longinus showed him a shortcut," she explained.

Longinus smiled broadly. "I saw how you jumped from the wall to the terraces, and it inspired a plan. I helped John get the Blessed Sacrament out onto the neighbor's rooftop." He pointed to the house next door on the right. "Then Gaspar got thrown into the Upper Room, so I untied him and we found the Blessed Mother downstairs, but by then we were all trapped inside."

"Gaspar told us you were facing Rabbi Malachi and the guards all by yourself," she said.

"Timon was there too—" I took off running to the side yard, and Timon was still lying at the bottom of the stairs.

The back of his head was swollen, but he was conscious. Longinus unchained him and he was able to sit up.

A huge pond had formed under the water tank, and Malachi and the guards were lying on their backs in the water, stunned. Only their faces stuck out. Malachi's phylactery was strapped between his rapidly blinking eyes. Muddy water droplets ran from his gray cheeks into the water around him. People came running out of the inn and surrounded him and the guards. I spotted the hitching post and retrieved my dagger from the water.

"How did this happen?" the Blessed Mother asked.

Everyone looked around, shrugging their shoulders, then Uncle Shem spoke from the back of the crowd. "I was just running up when I saw that the Pharisee and the guards were about to burn down the house." Uncle Shem came forward and patted me on the back. "Eli utterly vanquished them."

The crowd rushed toward me, cheering and shouting. A man the size and shape of a gladiator said, "You're a hero, young man."

Gaspar yelled, "Eli, you saved us!"

"And this holy place!" Ezra added.

Longinus strode over and saluted me. "You showed all the courage of an outcast."

Timon yelled over the jubilant outbursts, "Well done! I'm glad you had my dagger!"

My ears burned with embarrassment at being the center of attention. I wouldn't let their opinions define me, but I let myself enjoy the moment. My soul felt like it was soaring on a rope swing. And I had a feeling Jesus was pleased with me too.

The Blessed Mother put her hands on my shoulders. "Thank you from the bottom of my heart." Suddenly, she looked over my shoulder and her eyes sparkled.

John was walking up the street, carrying a monstrance with the Blessed Sacrament.

I let out a piercing whistle. When the festive crowd grew silent, I said, "Thank you, but truly all glory belongs to God." I dropped to my knees in the mud as the Blessed Sacrament approached. The Blessed Mother knelt at the exact same time. The rest of the crowd saw what was happening and immediately knelt. John carried the Blessed Sacrament up the steps and safely into the Upper Room. As soon as the door shut, the crowd cheered even louder.

CHAPTER 35

BEARING UNBURIED TREASURE

The moon shone in the pond beneath the water tank as we celebrated victory over our enemies, and our last night together. Uncle Shem's face reflected the light of the Son, whom he met that night. I was pretty sure Jesus smoothed out his dents with a planishing hammer.

Longinus bound Malachi and the guards' hands and feet and took them away in the wagon. Gaspar used his announcer voice to tell the entire Upper City how I defeated them.

The next morning, as we walked out of the Upper Room, the Blessed Mother pulled me aside. "I'm so happy you've decided to help bring our Jesus to the

233

world. Peter asked that I tell you where you're needed first. You'll travel with Gaspar's caravan until the last day of your journey, then the Apostle Thomas and the caravan will continue to Gaspar's country while John, Shem, and you head to Galilee."

"Galilee? Really?"

"You know that route well." Her lips and the crinkles at the corners of her eyes curved into smiles. "And I bet you know an innkeeper who would welcome Jesus."

"We can have the Breaking of Bread in my house?"

She nodded and I rushed in to hug her.

"I'll always be grateful to you," she said.

"Me? Because of you, I met Jesus. How can I ever thank you?" I asked.

"The love you give my Son is the best thank you."

I pulled away, then bent down and kissed the hem of her dress.

When I stood up, she laid her hands on my head, then traced a cross on my forehead. "May the Holy Spirit guide you and keep you safe."

We headed out to the yard where the men had just finished loading up the horses.

Along the way, I asked if we could stop and give Tamar food. Not only did John give her food, but he also healed her in the name of Jesus. Those glow-worms were going to miss her.

The horses covered a great distance each day. Every morning, John offered the Breaking of Bread, and every night we shared stories around the fire.

Uncle Shem always made sure the fire was roaring and was the first to ride ahead in the spots frequented by bandits, which assured me he'd be a good provider for Mama.

When we reached the place where we were going to part company, we stopped at a stream for the horses to get a drink. As the men exchanged goodbyes, I thanked Gaspar for the ride and said, "I hope to see you again sometime."

"Oh, you will." Gaspar handed me a scroll. "Be careful when you unroll it." Before I could ask any questions, he ran to his horse.

I unrolled the scroll and despite being careful, two objects fell out. Lying in the dirt like twinkling eyes were two emeralds, just as beautiful as the one I had found and returned to Herod, but even larger.

I picked them up and rubbed the glass-like surfaces, then read the scroll. Somehow, without even trying, I read it in Gaspar's accented voice.

> LET US MEET BACK IN JERUSALEM NEXT
> YEAR IN THE MONTH OF NISAN. TRADE
> ONE OF THE EMERALDS SO YOUR MAMA
> CAN RENT A DONKEY.
>
> GASPAR,
> YOUR BROTHER IN JESUS

I tucked the emeralds into the scroll and watched the caravan ride away. They headed north while John, Uncle Shem, and I walked westward. I smiled at the thought of seeing Mama and giving her the emeralds . . . and more importantly, the Treasure.

John and I traveled together as Treasure bearers for a long time. I was there when Roman leaders put him in a vat of boiling oil, and he miraculously survived. But that's a story for another day. Later they banished him to Patmos, a small Greek island. It certainly wasn't the lost city of Atlantis, but at least the Treasure could reappear there. I'd like to think that before he ate his ration of bread and water, John offered the Breaking of Bread, then spent hours and hours with Jesus.

Today, I stand here as an old man, looking down from the top of the Lighthouse of Alexandria. Before I head down for another journey across the sea, I circle around the balcony and something catches my attention. It's not Jupiter shining in the constellation Leo, or the firelight reflecting off the black waves.

Down on the ground, a huge treasure map unrolls before me. The map shows the known world surrounding the Great Sea, but there are also undiscovered lands stretching far beyond that. The land is cobalt blue and outlined in gold, and the seas are midnight blue. The map floats up off the ground and the ends curl back toward one another, forming a huge sphere. Then I realize I'm looking down on the earth. I always knew it wasn't flat.

I hear the confident words of Jesus coming from every direction:

I WILL BE WITH YOU
TO THE END OF THE AGE.

I must be seeing the future because even the far-away lands have already been visited by Treasure bearers. Instead of seeing Xs marking treasure, I see thousands and thousands of little red lights—lights from a multitude of sanctuary lamps proclaiming that Jesus lives on in the Blessed Sacrament.

Believe me when I tell you, you don't have to live in Israel in AD 33 to meet Jesus. But be forewarned, good Treasure hunters watch out for false imitations. You'll find the authentic Treasure near the red, glowing sanctuary lamp inside a Catholic church. Wherever you're living, whenever you're living, go discover the living Jesus for yourself.

Acknowledgments

I owe a debt of gratitude to so many people. First, all glory to God for His help and inspiration. A huge thanks to my husband Paul who supported and advised me in so many ways. My sons Dom and Drew were my first audience, and this story is dedicated to them. My parents imparted the gift of the Catholic faith and have always given unconditional love and support.

Vijaya Bodach provided honest feedback and advised me throughout the entire process. My beta readers Tina Jost; Bill and Fran Levay; Dominic Vaughan; and Michelle, Amelia, Stephen, and Joshua Needham encouraged me with their feedback and prayers. Deacon Vaughan patiently answered my theological questions, and Michele McCoy made sure my Latin was correct. Michelle Buckman, Michael Seagriff, and Erin Brown Conroy, generously took time from their amazing work to be advanced reviewers. Erin Brown Conroy's fictional writing courses at Homeschool Connections were THE single biggest influence on my development as a writer. Mark at Zaxby's always gave me a warm welcome (with chocolate chips) and a corner office.

I'm incredibly grateful to Erin Broestl and Jean Ann Schoonover-Egolf of Perpetual Light Publishing. They have a plethora of projects to choose from, and I'm humbled that they chose this one. They understood my vision and were amazing collaborators, gently suggesting brilliant ideas but also giving me autonomy. Jeanie's cover art is gorgeous, and to have her artistic genius for my story is such a blessing. Erin and Jeanie became mentors and friends, and this story is much better because of them. Generally, publishing moves at a glacial pace, but Perpetual Light Publishing moves at the speed of light.

Blessed Mother, St. John the Beloved, Blessed Carlo Acutis, Manuel Fodera, and John Sebastian, thank you for your intercession. Jesus, thank You for remaining with us to the end of time.

May the heart of Jesus, in the Most Blessed Sacrament, be praised, adored, and loved with grateful affection, at every moment, in all the tabernacles of the world, even to the end of time.

With gratitude,
Janeen Zaio

DISCUSSION QUESTIONS

The answers to these questions can be found after question 25. Students should not be graded on knowing all the answers because the answers to many of these questions can't be found in the story. The questions are designed to get students to think deeply, share ideas, and learn from the answers of others and the answers listed here.

Spoiler alert: These questions give away elements of the plot and should be discussed only after reading all the specified chapters for each set of questions.

CHAPTERS 1-10

1. The Church Fathers said that the Blessed Mother is the Ark of the New Covenant. State the similarities between the original Ark of the Covenant and the Blessed Mother to show how she is the Ark of the New Covenant.

2. What was Eli's mother referring to when she told Eli to go around Jericho because of Herod and John the Baptist?

CHAPTERS 11-20

3. God wanted Sabbath to be a joyful day for people to rest from their work and worship Him. Over time, some Israelite leaders added over fifteen hundred additional rules, prohibiting people from doing many things on Sabbath, and the fear of breaking the law made it harder for people

to enjoy the day. When Jesus healed a lame man on Sabbath, the Pharisees criticized Jesus for healing on Sabbath and accused the man of breaking the law because he picked up his mat. At the other extreme, Eli pointed out that some people worked on Sabbath and didn't seem concerned about keeping the day holy, even though it's one of the Ten Commandments. Today Christians observe Sabbath on Sundays. Do you think that most Christians keep the day holy according to the way God intended? How so?

4. Do you think Eli should have been able to keep the emerald in good conscience since he found it, or should he have returned it as soon as he realized it belonged to King Herod? When you saw that David wasn't concerned about getting the emerald back, did it make you feel that Eli should have kept it?

5. Eli wanted to see the Lighthouse of Alexandria, which was one of the Seven Wonders of the Ancient World. Later, as he looked at the Temple in Jerusalem, he commented that only Israel directed its engineering and artistic brilliance for the one true God. Look up the Seven Wonders of the Ancient World and explain which ones were built to honor God. This website may help:

https://www.worldatlas.com/articles/the-seven-won-ders-of-the-ancient-world.html

CHAPTERS 21-24

6. When Eli was in the Valley of Hinnom, he said that, like Jesus, he was going to die before he accomplished his mission. Do you think Jesus accomplished His mission?

7. In the beginning, Eli despised Romans but thought that devout Israelites could do no wrong. What changed his perception?

8. The inscription on the mirror, "We are only what we are in the eyes of God and nothing more," is paraphrased from a quote from St. John Vianney who lived from 1786-1859. Explain why you agree or disagree with this statement.

CHAPTERS 25-28

9. How did you feel when Jacob went to a chariot race instead of going with Eli to meet Jesus in the Blessed Sacrament? What motivated Jacob? What are some of the activities that people in our time choose to do on Sundays instead of attending Mass?

10. Some people leave the Catholic Church because they think the music or the activities at other churches are more fun. Some of these people think that they're receiving Jesus in communion at those churches. They don't realize that transubstantiation only occurs through Catholic priests.*

(Transubstantiation means that, at the moment of consecration, the substance of the bread is changed into Jesus's Body, Blood, Soul, and Divinity, even though the characteristics of the bread such as taste, smell, and appearance remain the same.) What are some things we can do to help people who have left the Church?

11. Eli said that if he had found out that Jesus had died before he left for Jerusalem, he might not have found the Treasure. Do you think that Eli would have come to believe in Christ's Real Presence in the Blessed Sacrament if he had heard about It from someone other than John and the Blessed Mother?

CHAPTERS 29-31

12. When Eli was about to meet Jesus in the Blessed Sacrament, he was concerned that he wasn't ready, but the Blessed Mother assured him his soul had never been more radiant. What can we do to make our souls radiant before we receive Him in the Eucharist?

13. Can you guess what famous author said this? "I put before you the one great thing to love on earth: the Blessed Sacrament." Hint: His books have become blockbuster movies.

14. What can you do to increase your zeal for the Eucharist?

15. Until 587 BC, the Ark of the Covenant was kept in the Temple behind a veil in a restricted area called the Holy of Holies. One priest could go into the Holy of Holies on the Day of Atonement, and God would hover above the Ark and speak with him. At the moment of Jesus's death, that veil was torn in two, showing that Jesus reconciled us to God, so now we can all be in the Divine Presence.

Today, some people claim that the Ark of the Covenant is locked away in a church in Ethiopia. Do you think we should investigate to find out if this is truly the Ark of the Covenant, or do you agree with Eli that the Ark is no longer needed because we have Jesus's Divine Presence in the Blessed Sacrament?

16. Eli said that being with Jesus in Eucharistic Adoration was like being finished by a planishing hammer. He explained that the planishing hammer removes all the marks made by other hammers and smooths the metal until you have a finely crafted piece. What do you think he meant by this?

17. Jesus called Eli a man of God, but Eli was only twelve years old. Do you think Eli became a man of God over the course of his journey? What do you think it takes to be a man or woman of God?

CHAPTERS 32-35

18. Eli advised good treasure hunters to watch out for false imitations. He said you'd find the authentic Treasure near a red sanctuary lamp inside a Catholic church. Explain why transubstantiation occurs in Catholic churches, and why the bread remains bread at other Christian denominations.

19. While other Christian churches have Jesus present in the Scripture and in the community, it's different than having Jesus alive in the tabernacle in Catholic churches. G.K. Chesterton explained that the Blessed Sacrament in Catholic churches provides us with an unparalleled opportunity to be spiritually and physically close to Jesus. He said, "It is the difference between saying the Spirit of God pervades the universe and saying Jesus Christ just walked into the room." Do you agree with Chesterton's analogy? Can you come up with another way to explain the difference?

20. So many Eucharistic miracles point to the reality of transubstantiation. Research Eucharistic miracles and write a few sentences about the one you find most fascinating. This website describes over 150 Eucharistic miracles that have taken place all over the world:

http://therealpresence.org/eucharst/mir/engl_mir.htm

21. That list of Eucharistic miracles was compiled by a modern-day Treasure bearer, Blessed Carlo Acutis. At the age of eleven, Carlo began researching stories of Eucharistic miracles from around the world, and within a few years, he had compiled the list of over 150 miracles. Go to this website dedicated to him and write down three interesting facts about his life. https://carloacutis-en.org/

22. We're all called to be Treasure bearers, telling others about Jesus's Real Presence. What are some fun activities your church groups can do that are centered around the Eucharistic Jesus?

23. Compare and contrast Shem's actions in the beginning with those of Longinus. What motivated the two men?

24. The disciples took the Blessed Sacrament all over the known world. What is the most exotic place that anyone has ever taken the Blessed Sacrament?

25. What do you think the treasure with a face is?

Answers to Discussion Questions

Chapters 1-10

1. The Blessed Mother is the Ark of the New Covenant for several reasons. The Ark contained manna, and the Blessed Mother held Jesus, the new manna, inside of her when she carried Him for nine months. In so doing, she carried the Word of God, and the Ark also contained the word of God, the Ten Commandments on stone tablets.

Wherever the Israelites took the Ark, whether it was in the middle of the army as they circled Jericho, inside a tabernacle (tent) in the desert, or in the Temple in Jerusalem, that's where God was present on earth. Similarly, God became present on earth through the Blessed Mother.

Until Jeremiah hid the Ark from the Babylonians, it had been kept in the Temple in Jerusalem; likewise, the Blessed Mother may have lived in the Temple for many years. An ancient writing and private revelations say that the Blessed Mother's parents took her to the Temple when she was two years old, and she may have lived and worked there until she became engaged to St. Joseph.

In Revelation 11:19-12:1, St. John the Apostle sees a vision of God's heavenly temple and the Ark of the Covenant. When John goes on to describe what he sees, instead of describing the golden box, he describes a woman clothed with the sun, with the moon under her feet, and a crown with twelve stars. Scholars agree it is the Blessed Mother.

2. One of King Herod's homes was in Jericho, and he was known for his violent behavior, including having John the Baptist beheaded. King Herod's father (King Herod the Great) was the one who had ordered the deaths of all the children under the age of two in Bethlehem when he heard from the Wise Men that the King of the Jews had been born there.

Chapters 11-20

3. Answers will vary.

4. As soon as Eli realized that the emerald belonged to Herod, he should have given it back. Even if Eli needed it more than Herod, it rightly belonged to Herod.

5. The Seven Wonders of the Ancient World were the Hanging Gardens of Babylon, the Statue of Zeus at Olympia, the Mausoleum at Halicarnassus, the Temple of Artemis, the Colossus of Rhodes, the Great Pyramid of Giza, and the Lighthouse of Alexandria. None of these Wonders of the World were built to glorify the one true God. In ancient times, only Israelites worshiped the one true God, and people of other countries worshiped false gods, but God intended for Israel to help other nations come to know Him. The moment

before Jesus ascended, He commissioned the disciples (who were mostly Israelites) to tell the world about Him.

Chapters 21-24

6. Yes, Jesus accomplished His mission. He came to die for our sins so that we have the opportunity to be reconciled with God.

7. Eli was prejudiced against Romans, but after Longinus helped him, Eli began to see that Romans could be kind and holy. Likewise, Eli's perception that all Israelites were good changed when he met Rabbi Malachi. Though Malachi was a respected leader and supposedly a devout Israelite, he turned out to be evil. All people are created equal in the eyes of God, so we should never be prejudiced toward groups of people. We need to see people as unique individuals and not make assumptions about them or put them into categories.

8. Answers will vary.

Chapters 25-28

9. Opinions will vary about how people felt when Jacob attended a chariot race instead of meeting Jesus. Jacob liked fun, action, and adventure. He had a competitive streak and was motivated by the desire to win at everything. His dream was to become a famous charioteer. Today, there are still

people like Jacob who place activities like sports, sleep, or entertainment over a relationship with Christ. We can pray for their conversion and show them how a relationship with Jesus brings us everlasting joy, not just fleeting enjoyment.

10. Answers will vary. Of course, we need to be kind to these people and never judgmental. Perhaps they were not taught about the Real Presence. We can watch for an opportunity to explain how Jesus is truly present in the Eucharist at Catholic churches.* We can start a conversation by showing a genuine interest in what they believe about communion at their new church. We can reference Bible verses about the Real Presence (such as John 6:48-57, 1 Corinthians 11:23-27, or 1 Corinthians 10:16). Perhaps we can invite them to attend Mass with us and before going into the church, briefly explain what will happen at the moment of consecration. We can also give them books about the Eucharist and pray that the Holy Spirit will enlighten them.

Other church services may include praise music or entertainment that makes us feel good, but Fr. Mike Schmitz said that worship is not about what we get out of it, but rather what we can give to God. Jesus taught the disciples how to offer the Holy Sacrifice of the Mass, in which we re-present His sacrifice to God, so it makes sense that we would give Him the kind of worship that He wants. We can also sing praise music during Mass or at activities outside of Mass.

Lastly, we can make sure our youth group activities are fun and appealing to others.

Please see Answer 18 about transubstantiation also occurring through Orthodox priests at Orthodox churches.

11. Answers will vary.

Chapters 29-31

12. When the priest holds up the Consecrated Host, we can say the centurion's prayer with sincerity. "Lord, I am not worthy that You should enter under my roof but only say the word, and my soul shall be healed." We should avoid sin and go to Confession frequently. We should not receive the Eucharist until we've confessed any mortal sins.

As Eli went up to receive the Eucharist, the Blessed Mother was behind him, and he felt she was vouching for him. We can also ask her to escort us up to Jesus, so that we can be more acceptable to Him. St. Louis de Montfort recommended that we ask the Blessed Mother to loan us her Immaculate Heart before we receive Jesus. As we're walking up the aisle, we can be mindful that It's Jesus, so that we're never just going through the motions.

13. J.R.R. Tolkien, the author of *The Lord of the Rings* series, said that about the Blessed Sacrament.

14. Answers will vary, but here are some ideas: Go to Eucharistic Adoration and Mass as often as possible, or at least try to stop by a Catholic church for a quick visit with Jesus every day. Whenever you're in church and your mind wanders, remind yourself that Jesus is truly present. After receiving Holy Communion, remind yourself that Jesus is within you and speak to Him heart-to-heart.

Pray that Jesus will give you zeal for the Eucharist. This prayer by St. Thomas More is very helpful:

I wish, my Lord, to receive You, with the purity, humility, and devotion, with which Your most holy mother received You, with the spirit and fervor of the saints.

15. Answers will vary. It's interesting to note that in 2 Maccabees 2:5-8 when Jeremiah hid the Ark of the Covenant in a cave, the people who followed him wanted to mark the trail leading to the exact location, but they couldn't find it. Jeremiah said to them, "The place is to remain unknown until God gathers His people together again and shows them mercy." Has the time of God's mercy already come, allowing the Ethiopians to find the Ark, or will we find it at some point in the future? Sadly in 2020, while war was being waged in Ethiopia, soldiers attacked the church where the Ark is allegedly hidden. Villagers came to help, and over 750 of them reportedly died, but they were able to prevent the soldiers from stealing the alleged Ark.

16. Uncle Shem had criticized and insulted Eli, destroying his confidence. During adoration, Jesus showed Eli that He valued him, healing the pain from Uncle Shem's insults and helping Eli regain his sense of worth.

17. Answers will vary.

Chapters 32-35

18. A Catholic priest can consecrate the bread because he's been validly ordained by a bishop who comes from a long line of bishops stemming directly from the twelve Apostles and Jesus Himself. We call this Apostolic Succession.

Though Eli didn't mention the Orthodox churches because they didn't exist in his lifetime, Orthodox priests can also consecrate the bread. They have Apostolic Succession, and their sacraments are valid but illicit. Orthodox churches are in a schism with the pope, but the Catechism of the Catholic Church states that while they are in an imperfect communion with the Catholic Church, "this communion is so profound that it lacks little to attain the fullness that would permit a common celebration of the Lord's Eucharist." (Catechism of the Catholic Church. Second Edition. English translation. Vatican City: Libreria Editrice Vaticana, 1994. Print. section 838.)

Starting in the sixteenth century, a few men left the Catholic Church and began their own churches, breaking the chain of Apostolic Succession so their priests or ministers cannot consecrate the bread. Today there are thousands of these Christian denominations, such as Baptists, Lutherans, Methodists, and Presbyterians, without the Real Presence in the Eucharist.

One word of caution: Anglican churches have a tabernacle and a sanctuary lamp but not the Real Presence. Anglicans belong to the Church of England which was started by King Henry VIII. In 1533, when the pope refused to let King Henry divorce his wife and marry another woman, King Henry cut ties with the Catholic Church and forced priests to recognize him as the head of the church in England. Then his son Edward changed the ordination rite in a way that made it invalid. Since that time, any Anglican priest ordained with that rite can't consecrate the bread.

19. Answers will vary.

20. Answers will vary. A fascinating miracle took place in India in 2001. Before the Holy Sacrifice of the Mass began, a priest opened the tabernacle and saw the image of a human face in the Consecrated Host. He asked the altar server what he saw, and the altar server confirmed that he saw the face too. The congregation began kneeling in adoration, and the image of the face became clearer, resembling Jesus wearing the crown of thorns. You can see the picture at this website:

https://www.churchpop.com/2020/01/23/holy-face-of-jesus-allegedly-appears-on-eucharistic-host-in-india/

21. Answers will vary, but here are some facts about Blessed Carlo Acutis. He was very talented at computer programming and web design. He developed a website describing the Eucharistic miracles, then designed an exhibit which was later made into the book *Vatican International Exhibition of The Eucharistic Miracles of the World.* After his First Holy Communion, Carlo went to Mass every single day and put the Eucharist at the center of his life, calling it his "highway to heaven." One time he said, "If Jesus remains with us always, wherever there is a Consecrated Host, what need is there to make a pilgrimage to visit the places where Jesus lived 2000 years ago?"

Sadly, Carlo died of leukemia in 2006 at the age of fifteen. Pope Francis advanced his cause for sainthood and declared him Blessed in 2020. After asking for Carlo's intercession, a boy in Brazil was miraculously healed from a disorder that prevented him from eating solid foods. Ask Blessed Carlo Acutis to intercede for you and your intentions.

22. Answers will vary, but here's one idea. Our parish has Eucharistic Adoration the entire night before First Friday, so our homeschooling group used to have adoration campouts. After evening Mass on Thursday, each family set up a tent in the yard across from church. Then we'd have s'mores around

a campfire and play games. At bedtime, each family went to its tent, then throughout the night, people took turns walking over to church and spending an hour with Jesus. It was a fun way to get people to try adoration.

23. Both Shem and Longinus were skilled in their professions and had pride in their native countries, but they were different in the way they treated others. Uncle Shem yelled at Eli, called him Slapdash, and insulted him for being clumsy. Uncle Shem considered himself a devout Israelite, but he didn't live the Israelite values of kindness and compassion. Shem was driven by the desire to rebuild his reputation and gain fame for being the first Israelite to make a mirror out of glass. (The name Shem means fame, reputation, or name). Though Eli broke the first mirror by accident, Uncle Shem reacted with anger instead of patience, understanding, and forgiveness. He was also reluctant to follow Jesus because he was afraid of what people would think of him if Jesus turned out to be another false messiah. The character Longinus was based on St. Longinus, the Roman soldier who put the spear in Jesus's side at the Resurrection. In this fictional story, Longinus was kind, even going out of his way to help Eli, who was a stranger. Longinus had just become a Christian and was motivated to live the Christian values. He said that even Romans didn't understand him, implying that other Romans may have criticized him for becoming Christian, but he didn't let that stop him from openly following Jesus.

Optional activity: Research the real story of St. Longinus to see how he was persecuted and tortured for his Catholic faith.

24. The most exotic place anyone has ever taken the Blessed Sacrament is outer space. In 1994, three astronauts received the Eucharist while on the Space Shuttle Endeavor. One of the astronauts said that what happened immediately after they received the Eucharist was truly moving. "As we meditated quietly in the darkened cockpit, a dazzling white light burst through space and into the cabin. Pure radiance from the risen sun streamed through Endeavour's forward cockpit windows and bathed us in its warmth. What else could this be but a sign? — God's gentle affirmation of our union with Him." This story came from the book *Sky Walking: An Astronaut's Memoir* written by the astronaut Dr. Tom Jones.

25. In the beginning, some people may have thought the Treasure with a face was the mirror because a mirror has a face. Others may have thought it was the Ark of the Covenant because it was topped with statues of angels. Actually, the author was referring to the Blessed Sacrament as the Treasure with a face. While we don't see Jesus's face when we look at the Consecrated Host, It is the living Jesus.

Father John Hardon spoke about how the Eucharistic

Jesus is the living Jesus. He said, "Jesus is on earth in the Blessed Sacrament. Why? In order that we might come to Him now no less frequently than His contemporaries did in first-century Palestine. If we thus approach Him in loving faith, there is no limit to the astounding things He will do. Why not? In the Eucharist, He has the same human lips that told the raging storm, 'Be still,' and commanded the dead man, "Lazarus, come forth.' "

Glossary

For vocabulary words and other resources,
please visit **JaneenZaio.com.**

CHAPTER 1

The Great Sea – ancient name for the Mediterranean Sea.

Persian (PURR-zhun) – a person from Persia, a country in southwestern Asia. In 1935, the country changed its name to Iran.

Nisean Horse (nigh-SEE-uhn) – the most valuable breed of horses in ancient times. These horses were known for their beauty, elegance, and the characteristic bony knobs on their foreheads, referred to as horns. Persian nobles and military leaders rode them.

Peace Be Upon You – an Israelite greeting. The Hebrew word shalom means "peace be upon you."

Behistun Rock (bee-HISS-tuhn) – a huge rock carving on the side of Mount Behistun in modern-day Iran. It was commissioned by King Darius of Persia in 520 BC and features a sculpture of him standing with a boot on his prostrate enemy while nine other rebels stand behind with ropes around their necks. Above the relief were inscriptions written in three different languages. People referred to it as *Treasure Story* and believed it told the secret of a great treasure. In 1843, a man scaled the cliff and translated the inscriptions which turned out to be a biography of King Darius; however, it was of great value to archaeologists because by comparing the three different languages, they were able to finally decipher ancient cuneiform writing.

Tunic (TOO-nik) – a type of clothing made by sewing two squares together and leaving a hole for the head. It reached the knees, had no sleeves, and was tied with a belt made of rope, leather, or cloth. Wealthy people wore tunics that extended to the ankles and had sleeves.

Planishing Hammer (PLAN-ish-ing) – a hammer with a slightly curved or flat face. After shaping a piece of metal, metalsmiths gently tap it with a planishing hammer to smooth out dents and imperfections.

Sixth Hour – the time from about noon until 1:00 p.m. The Israelites counted twelve hours of the day, starting at dawn and ending at sundown. The days are longer during the summer, so sometimes each hour was longer than sixty minutes.

CHAPTER 2

Malachite (MAL-uh-kite) – a green mineral that contains copper and is used for making pigment and ornamental objects.

Lighthouse of Alexandria – a lighthouse built in 280 BC. Standing at about four hundred feet high, it was one of the tallest structures in the ancient world. A fire burned brightly at the top to help guide ships into the harbor at Alexandria, Egypt. The lighthouse was destroyed by earthquakes in the thirteenth century, but today scuba divers can still see the ruins in the harbor.

Israelites (IZ-ree-uh-lites) – descendants of the patriarch Jacob that formed the nation of Israel. Israelites were also referred to as Hebrews in ancient times, or as Israelis or Jews today.

Heathen (HEE-thuhn) – an ancient term for a person who did not believe in the one, true God.

Acacia (uh-KAY-shuh) – any of numerous shrubs and trees of the legume family that grow in warm areas and have white or yellow flower clusters.

The Day of Atonement (uh-TONE-muhnt) – the most important day of the year for Israelites. They fasted, prayed, and asked God to forgive the sins they committed over the past year. In ancient times, the high priest put his hands on the head of a goat, symbolically putting the people's sins on it, then sent it out into the wilderness. The priest sacrificed another goat and sprinkled its blood on the Ark of the Covenant. Jews still observe the feast today, and it is also known as Yom Kippur.

Holy of Holies (HO-lee uv HO-leez) – the innermost and most sacred room of the Temple in Jerusalem. No one was permitted to enter except for one priest on the Day of Atonement. The Ark of the Covenant was kept in the Holy of Holies.

CHAPTER 3

Passover (PASS-oh-ver) – A holy day in which Israelites remember how God instructed their ancestors to put blood on their doorposts, so that the Angel of Death would pass over their houses as he killed the firstborn sons of the Egyptians. That night, God led the Israelites out of slavery in Egypt. During Jesus's time, Israelites traveled to Jerusalem to celebrate Passover by sacrificing a lamb at the Temple and eating it with their families.

CHAPTER 4

Cloak (klohk) – a large square cloth worn over a tunic that was used to keep out the rain or cold wind and as a blanket at night. It could be draped over the shoulders, pulled up over the head, or used to carry things. It is also referred to as a mantle.

Galley (GAL-ee) – a large, low ship of ancient times moved by oars and sails. Sometimes slaves were chained to the oars and forced to row.

Nisan (NEE-sahn) – the first month in the Jewish calendar which coincides with March and April in the Gregorian, or Christian calendar of today.

CHAPTER 7

Amphitheater (AM-fuh-thee-uh-ter) – an oval or circular structure with tiers of seats arranged around an open space. People performed plays or gave speeches in the open space.

CHAPTER 10

Shekel (SHEK-uhl) – a silver coin weighing four-tenths of an ounce. A shekel was the basic unit of money in ancient Israel.

Aramaic (ar-uh-MAY-ik) – a language spoken by the Israelites. In Jesus's time, the Israelites spoke Hebrew in the synagogues and the Temple, but Aramaic in everyday communications.

CHAPTER 11

Mica (MY-kuh) – any of various minerals that contain silicon and can easily be separated into thin, often transparent sheets.

CHAPTER 12

Shevat (shuh-VAHT) – the eleventh month in the Jewish calendar which coincides with January and February in the Gregorian, or Christian calendar of today.

Cubit (KYOO-bit) – an ancient unit of length based on the length of the forearm from the elbow to the tip of the middle finger, and equal to about eighteen inches.

CHAPTER 14

Yoke (yohk) – a device for joining a pair of draft animals, especially oxen, usually consisting of a crosspiece with two bow-shaped pieces, each enclosing the head of an animal.

Fringe (frinj) – a decorative border of thread or cord, usually hanging loosely from a raveled edge or separate strip. God instructed the Israelites to wear fringes on the four corners of their cloaks as a symbol of their obedience to His commands.

Pharisee (FAIR-uh-see) – a member of a Jewish sect noted for its strict observance of rites and ceremonies of the written law, and for its insistence on the validity of the group's own oral traditions concerning the law.

CHAPTER 20

Valley of Hinnom (VAL-ee uhv HIN-uhm) – a valley surrounding Jerusalem where the garbage was taken and burned. In the Old Testament, the prophet Jeremiah wrote about the evil actions of people who lit fires in the valley and sacrificed their children to a false god. The Greek name of the valley is Gehenna.

Bar (bahr) – an Aramaic word meaning "son of." In ancient Israel, a man could be referred to by his first name, then bar, then his father's name. An example is Simon bar Jonah, which is Simon, son of Jonah.

Consiste (cohn-SEE-stay) – the Latin word for halt or stop moving.

Publican (PUHB-li-kuhn) – a person who collects tribute, taxes, or tolls.

CHAPTER 21

Wax Seal – a piece of wax with a raised impression of an emblem, symbol, or word. It is used as proof of authority.

Longinus (Lawn-JIE-nuhs) – the name of a Roman soldier in this story, inspired by St. Longinus who put the spear in Jesus's side at the crucifixion.

Phylactery (fi-LAK-tuh-ree) – a small square leather box containing Scripture passages on slips of paper. During morning prayers, Israelite men wore a phylactery on their left arm and their forehead.

CHAPTER 22

Mikveh (MIK-vuh) – a pool in which Israelites immersed themselves to become ritually purified.

CHAPTER 23

Circus (SUR-kuhs) – a large oval, roofless building with tiered seats around an open space. It was used for chariot races, public games, and naval reenactments. Another term for a circus is coliseum.

Sanhedrin (San-HEH-druhn) – the supreme council of the Israelites, consisting of seventy-one members, including a high priest. The Sanhedrin was responsible for interpreting religious and civil laws.

CHAPTER 24

Naval Reenactment (NAY-vuhl ree-uh-NAKT-ment) – an event in which Romans filled the circus with water and had criminals simulate famous battles that happened at sea.

CHAPTER 26

Seven-branched Candlestick – an ornate candlestick consisting of a central shaft and three pairs of branches curving upward from out of the shaft. It is also known as a menorah.

CHAPTER 27

Mount Vesuvius (vuh-SOOH-vee-uhs) – an active volcano in southwestern Italy. One of its largest eruptions occurred in AD 79, destroying Pompeii and several other cities.

CHAPTER 28

Nevi'im (Neh-vee-EEM) – the second part of the Jewish Scriptures which contains the writings of the prophets.

The Breaking of Bread – the original name of the Holy Sacrifice of the Mass. Acts 2:42 states that the followers of Jesus, " . . . devoted themselves to the Apostles' teaching and fellowship, to the breaking of bread and the prayers."

CHAPTER 30

Hallel Psalm (hah-LEYL sahm) – a liturgical prayer consisting of all or part of Psalms 113–118. It was recited on Passover and other Jewish feasts.

CHAPTER 31

The Tribe of Judah (JOO-duh) – descendants from Judah, a son of Jacob. The country of Israel was made up of twelve tribes descending from Jacob.

CHAPTER 33

Exodus (EKS-uh-duhs) – the rescue of Moses and the Israelites from slavery in Egypt. As God led the people out, He parted the Red Sea into two walls of water, so the Israelites could walk through on dry land, then He let the walls of water crash down on the pursuing Egyptians.

CHAPTER 35

Monstrance (MAHN-struhnts) – a metal holder in which the Blessed Sacrament is exposed for veneration at Benediction or Eucharistic Adoration, or in which It is carried during a procession.

Patmos (PAT-mohs) – a Greek island where the Apostle John was exiled and saw the vision that he wrote about in Revelation.

END NOTES

Although the Blessed Mother, St. John, St. Longinus, and St. Peter were real people, their words and actions in this story are fictional. (Of course, St. John really did survive being put in a vat of boiling oil!) When the Blessed Mother and St. John explain how the bread truly becomes Jesus at the consecration, many of their words were taken from the Gospels and paraphrased. The exact Bible verses are referenced below. All of the other characters have been created by the author, and any resemblance to other people is coincidental.

All Bible verses except where noted come from *The New American Bible*. St. Joseph Ed. New York: Catholic Book Publishing, 1970. Print.

Chapter 2
Eli's dad inscribed this quote on his slingshot:
"Take courage and be a man." 1 Kings 2:2

Chapter 7
Uncle Shem recites this psalm at the Todah:

"For my soul has been freed from death, my eyes from tears, and my feet from stumbling. I shall walk before the Lord in the land of the living." Psalm 116, *The Holy Bible.* Rev. Standard Ed. Catholic Ed. San Francisco: Ignatius Press, 1966. Print.

Chapter 24

The quote inscribed on the mirror is paraphrased from St. John Vianney:

"My children, we are in reality only what we are in the eyes of God and nothing more." Vianney, St. John. *Thoughts of the Curé D'Ars.* Charlotte: TAN Books, 1984. Print.

Chapter 27

St. John and the Blessed Mother paraphrase these Bible verses when they speak about the Eucharist:

"Go, therefore, and make disciples of all nations, baptizing them in the name of the Father, and of the Son, and of the Holy Spirit, teaching them to observe all that I have commanded you. And behold, I am with you always, until the end of the age." Matthew 28:19-20

"This is My Body which will be given for you; do this in memory of Me." Luke 22:19

"This cup which is poured out for you is the New Covenant in My Blood." Luke 22:20

" . . . the bread that I will give is My Flesh for the life of the world." John 6:51

"Jesus said to them, 'Amen, amen, I say to you, unless you eat the Flesh of the Son of Man and drink His Blood, you do not have life within you. Whoever eats My Flesh and drinks My Blood has eternal life, and I will raise him on the last day. For My Flesh is true food and My Blood is true drink. Whoever eats My Flesh and drinks My Blood remains in Me and I in him.' " John 6:53-56

Chapter 28

Eli remembers this quote that he learned in school:
" . . . the Messiah will begin to be revealed . . . and those who are hungry will enjoy themselves, and they will, moreover, see marvels every day . . . manna will come down again from on high and they will eat of it . . . " This

is 2 Baruch 29:3, 6-8 in *The Apocalypse of Baruch,* which is an ancient Jewish text that is not in the Catholic Bible. Charlesworth, James, editor. *The Old Testament Pseudepigrapha.* Peabody: Hendrickson Publishers, 2010. Print.

Chapter 30
St. Peter references this Bible verse in his homily: "Thus says the Lord God who gathers the outcasts of Israel, 'I will gather others to Him besides those already gathered.'" Isaiah 56:8; *The Holy Bible.* Rev. Standard Ed. Catholic Ed. San Francisco: Ignatius Press, 1966. Print.

Chapter 31
Gaspar's explanation of the Star of Bethlehem comes from the details found here: https://catholicstraightanswers. com/three-kings-truth-behind-star/ and is based on findings from Roger Sinnott who cited evidence from Bryant Tuckeman's book *Planetary, Lunar and Solar Positions, 601 BC to AD 1.*

About the Author

Janeen Zaio is a retired homeschooling mom whose passion is encouraging devotion to Christ's Real Presence in the Eucharist. She has two grown sons and lives in South Carolina with her husband Paul and her dog Tula.

Though she savors her quiet time with the Blessed Sacrament, she also enjoys rowdy adventures. She travels throughout the Southeast, hosting the *Escape With the Ark Challenge* in which children solve clues and tackle obstacles in their own hunt for the Ark of the Covenant. It's like an escape room but without the walls—though you just might spot the walls of ancient Jerusalem.

Janeen is available to speak to parents about helping children have zeal for the Real Presence, and to church groups about ways to be ambassadors for the Real Presence. If you'd like her to host an adventure or speak to your group, please contact her at **JaneenZaio.com.** You can also follow her on Facebook:

The Treasure With a Face by Janeen Zaio

Janeen Zaio, Ambassadors for
Christ's Real Presence

Or on MeWe: **Catholics Who Love the Eucharist**

To learn more about the Blessed Sacrament or participating in an Escape With the Ark Challenge, visit **JaneenZaio.com**.

We hope you've enjoyed this book! If so, please be sure to leave a review at your favorite book-reviewing site.

www.perpetuallightpublishing.com

CPSIA information can be obtained
at www.ICGtesting.com
Printed in the USA
BVHW070956041021
618092BV00001B/70